"Something extraordinary is happening i
Cee-Cee has visions of angels and missing cnuaren. But after Cee-Cee performs a miracle, she's placed under the care of a radical group of nuns. Darkly beautiful, *Girls* examines how forgiveness and wisdom take hold in the most unexpected places." —*People*

"This debut sparkles; *Miracle Girls* is that rarest thing: a literary miracle. MB Caschetta will break your heart and mend it all at once."
—Darin Strauss, author of *Chang and Eng* and *Half a Life*

"What MB Caschetta's novel brilliantly proposes is an underground railroad for girls. It feels like one of those girls grew up and wrote *Miracle Girls*. I loved reading it and rooting for Cee-Cee as she struggles to survive her own family and her saintly little girl voyage with the aid of intergenerational healing, and the vintage magic of radical nuns and priests from a time when they worked for peace and helped the lost girls of the world find home." —Eileen Myles, *Chelsea Girls*

"It's not every day the Virgin Mary makes an appearance in a novel. And how fitting that MB Caschetta invites her into a story where a grandmother provides safety and thousands of prayers; where law-breaking nuns save desperate girls; where life hurts and is full of grace; a world where miracles happen. MB doesn't flinch from writing painful truths nor does she flinch from lifting her characters up and us along with them."
—Beverly Donofrio, *Riding in Cars with Boys*, *Looking for Mary*, and *Astonished*

"A wondrous and exhilarating novel. The Bianco family is unforgettable in all its catastrophic dysfunction but also in the capacity of some of its most broken members to fight their way toward salvation. *Miracle Girls* is an unflinching, fantastical and unexpectedly healing act of the imagination. You won't have read anything quite like it, and you're not likely soon to forget it either."
—Paul Russell, *Immaculate Blue* and *The Unreal Life of Sergey Nabokov*

"Has ten year old Cee-Cee Bianco just worked a miracle? Are her visions divine or or only the half-baked imaginings of a silly girl? Cee-Cee's mother has abandoned the family; her brother lies in a coma. Alone, she must pick her way through a wasteland of adult foolishness, but the intuitive wisdom that guides her seems an earthly miracle. Caschetta's vivid, thoughtful novel leaps, skips and soars along the boundary between faith and superstition, turning every expectation on its head."
—Heidi Jon Schmidt, *The Harbormaster's Daughter*

"*Miracle Girls* is a wondrous book in which gritty reality alternates with ecstatic visions, cruelty is leavened by grace, and the treachery of families and is redeemed by the kindness of strangers. MB Caschetta conjures an era, a place, and her characters unforgettably. An accomplished and exceptional debut novel."
—Ralph Sassone, *The Intimates*

"A polished debut novel…Caschetta's first novel is filled with a kind of dark poetry and the menace of ordinary evils." —*Kirkus Reviews*

"One gets the sense Caschetta offers her readers an idealized version of the Catholic Church as a safe-haven for all people, and where strict interpretation of the Bible goes both ways. I'm not sure this utopia is actually attainable, but within the world of *Miracle Girls*, you can almost believe it." —*LitReactor, BookShots*

"A mesmerizing first novel." —*Huffington Post*

"Compulsively readable first novel…*Miracle Girls* is an intriguing blend—part exploration of family ties, part exploration of what faith can look like, part radical concept, part history—and Caschetta does a wonderful job of weaving it all together. Her snappy prose, diverse cast of characters, and imaginative plot make *Miracle Girls* a pleasure to read. —*Lambda Literary Review*

"MB Caschetta's *Miracle Girls* is a stunning debut novel about an unforgettable dysfunctional family and faith." —*Largehearted Boy*

PRETEND

I'M

YOUR

FRIEND

PRETEND

I'M

YOUR

FRIEND

stories

MB CASCHETTA

EB

Engine Books

Indianapolis

Engine Books
PO Box 44167
Indianapolis, IN 46244
enginebooks.org

10 9 8 7 6 5 4 3 2 1

ISBN: 978-1-938126-42-0

Library of Congress Control Number: 2016934979

For Meryl

TABLE OF CONTENTS

HANDS

OF

GOD

HANDS OF GOD

HELENA FRANKEL HAS THE squarest teeth A. J. Wojak has ever seen.

It strikes her as odd to realize this now of all times, well into their third mid-Atlantic hour of flight to a place neither has been before—though, really, neither has been anywhere. Helena is the most beautiful girl in all of Waynesboro, Pennsylvania, place of their birth, and exactly *nowhere*. And yet, in the back of A.J.'s mind, she's started to realize she's growing bored in their friendship, antsy. The thought is nearly unthinkable. So A.J. revises: She is growing bored with Helena's breakup saga, which has been the topic of conversation nonstop since boarding the plane at five this morning.

Neither here nor there, A.J. thinks wistfully, looking out at clouds.

Before today, Helena had spoken in absolute terms: "Italy! Finally!"

She and Helena saved up money for two years, arranged the timing of this trip carefully, sorting out A.J.'s high school vacation and Helena's holiday work schedule at the factory's administrative office.

Maybe the real problem is that A.J. is no longer stoned, which means she is irritated, which means she should suggest a trip to the bathroom, which she will do as soon as she can get a word in edgewise.

In the meantime, her slow, buzzing mind has lazily landed on the nature of bicuspids. Helena's are bone white, perfectly rounded for the tearing of flesh, though she is strictly vegetarian, which A.J. admires. Also, due to a slight speech impediment, even the hardest consonants slipping from Helena's lips are wet and smooth. It's a pleasant sound, Helena talking, if you can loosen your mind around the tedious content.

The problem is timing: two days before their departure, Helena discovered her boyfriend, Gordon Johnson, a foreman at the P&G, in bed with someone else.

"Not just someone," Helena says, reviewing the facts. "But two someones! I mean, Gordy was in bed with *a couple*, A.J.—a girl *and* her husband."

Helena clutches the love note she found stuffed in Gordy's wallet, which almost caused her to cancel first the relationship and then the trip. The only trouble was that a) she is in love with Gordy, and b) Easter is the only week she can take off work without it affecting her paycheck.

Procter & Gamble is closed Holy Thursday, Good Friday, and the following Monday.

There is a world, A.J. tells herself, *a wide, wide world.*

"I mean, a threesome, A.J.!" Helena says. "A married couple with a baby and everything!"

Helena is wearing jeans that pinch her boyish hips and angle way out at the ankle. There's a rip in her turtleneck sweater, which is cream-colored and nearly matches her skin. A.J. marvels that Helena's father let her out of the house that way. When she thinks of her own father—a guy who drives a school bus, who was once unanimously elected to town council, and who makes a mean gin martini—her mind goes blank. Her body produces a numb floating sensation, as if she's stoned, as if the very thought of his existence wipes hers out entirely.

A.J.'s father let her travel mostly because of Helena: *People can say what they will about the Jews, but Helena Frankel is good people, a darn pretty little thing.* It's true that Helena is Jewish, but no one in Waynesboro treats her like it. Besides, the Frankels have been part of the town since the beginning; they've owned the drug store on East Main for as long as anyone can remember.

Helena grimaces, twisting her lips strangely and wiping away tears. A.J. has to squint to detect in her the senior voted Most Likely to Succeed, Class of '72.

Helena lowers her voice. "He'd go there for dinner, and after the kid was in bed, they lit a fire in the fireplace and the three of them had sex—all together at the same time—in the living room. He told me that, A.J."

A.J. is impressed with the idea that a regular guy like Gordy Johnson might not be so regular. A.J. can close her eyes and practically see Gordy, his tall angular body, his weird yellow hair, huffing and puffing for the pleasure of some bored faceless housewife and her not-so-bored faceless husband. Accidentally for a minute she imagines Helena there, too, naked on the rug next to Gordy. She opens her eyes and stares at a woman sleeping across the aisle, realizing the picture is wrong. *Too many people.*

In her backpack, she has some marijuana, rolled and ready to go, which they will smoke if Helena ever shuts up about Gordy's perversions.

"But did Gordy actually have *sex* with the guy?" A.J. asks. "I mean, together?"

Helena pulls back a handful of curly red hair and tucks it in her collar. "That's what I've been trying to tell you. The guy'd been in Vietnam, and Gordy felt guilty because he couldn't go to war on account of all that mental stuff from his past. The war was like a connection Gordy had with this guy. They were both messed up about it—the guy because he went, and Gordy because he couldn't go."

"Oh," A.J. says.

It is 1973, she reminds herself, the year of her graduation. In two short months, she'll be working at the P&G like everyone else, and maybe then she'll have the story to tell.

"I'd be messed up too," A.J. says, "if I had to go to Vietnam."

Helena bites down hard on an airline coffee cup. "Stupid fucking war."

She would like Helena to name a few names: Gordy Johnson's faceless couple, to be exact. But she decides not to press, since Helena can be touchy, and they've got a solid week ahead of them in Florence, Venice, and Rome. Anyway, it's easy enough in a small town to find out who someone like Gordy is fucking. To remind herself that everything's different now that they've left Pennsylvania, A.J. occupies her mind with thoughts of ancient ruins, and pungent nightclubs, and not-quite-sanitary youth hostels.

"Gordon said having that guy's dick inside him brought him back to life," Helena whispers.

A.J. imagines Gordy's ass in the air, not quite sure whether she's in favor or against. "Well, free love," she says, trying to sound poetic.

"Man, you can say that again."

A.J. waves her beaded bag of joints in the air. "Bathroom?"

Helena nods, getting up slowly and making her way toward the slim area of tiny restrooms at the back of the plane. Knocking her hip into the seats, she disturbs not one but two sleeping women with infants in their arms, who look up, surprised, and clutch their babies tighter. A.J. smiles apologetically as she follows: Helena is merely trying to exact revenge against the half of a couple that's breaking her heart. At the back of the cabin, Helena nods toward a stewardess in a blue jersey who saunters down the opposite aisle. "Wait till she passes. I'll leave it unlatched."

The stewardess raises an eyebrow at A.J., a thinly-plucked question mark. A.J. waves innocently, ducking inside and locking the door.

"Coast is clear," she says.

In the cramped space above the sink, A.J. produces a joint, lighting it quickly and taking two long, deep drags, which burn her lungs and feel good. She eventually lets the smoke waft out and the sweet tingling sensation wade in. Against her closed eyelids is an imprint of weird Gordy Johnson with his tongue in some man's mouth.

Waiting her turn, Helena muses, "When we get to Italy, let's fuck guys like crazy."

A.J. nods, holding out the joint for Helena's remarkable mouth, which is thin at the corner and wide toward the middle, a spoon. Gracefully, the top pink lip touches and releases the bottom pink lip as Helena leans in for a hit.

At a hostel next to the Pitti Palace, they drop off their bags and smoke a joint with some Italians. Then Helena grabs A.J.'s hand, and they start off toward the old center. A.J. concentrates on a tourist map of the ancient city. At first sight Florence is disappointing. It is smallish and blunt, yellowy-gold, the color of a stubbed-out cigarette.

A nicotine stain, A.J. thinks.

There's never any way to anticipate the imperfections of a place. Perhaps the future will merely be a series of letdowns, proving the only real location is in the mind. She bites her nails and rustles the map.

What if it's me?

Here she is: girl in a golden city, still seeing the world with Waynesboro eyes. Though how else would A.J. Wojak ever view the world? If not through her own eyes, then whose?

"Come on," Helena grabs the map where it folds. "We don't need this thing."

Helena's breath is a peppermint airplane candy.

"Give it up." She laughs, then threads her arm through A.J.'s and pulls her along. "I can't stand how beautiful this place is!"

A.J. agrees: Florence is far better than anything they've ever seen. Still, the difference between here and there is small and disturbing. *What if it's essentially the same wherever you are?* She longs to be lifted up and out of her own tedious mind, her lumpy, too-big body. As Helena weaves them around two old women selling trinkets on a long arching bridge, she considers how small the difference is between being alive and being dead, being herself and not herself.

Infinitesimal, she wants to say aloud. The thought gives her a chill.

Helena would tell her not to overthink it. Once Gordy had overthought peas, Helen had told her: For months all he could talk about was their size, their shape, the different colors they came in. When you thought about peas long enough, he'd claimed, you could no longer imagine anything more powerful. The exercise had landed him in the county hospital.

A.J. makes a mental note: *Steer clear of peas.*

"Wow," Helena giggles, still stoned. "I think I'm going to explode. I mean, look at that, will you?" She points to the first of many Davids they will see during the week.

A.J. snaps a photo of the statue and begins to relax a little, letting Helena's enthusiasm carry her forward. Her fingers are laced loosely in Helena's hands. The cool temperature of her skin is comforting.

When they arrive at the next place, Helena throws her arms around A.J.'s hips. "I want my life to be like this always," she says. "You and me and Florence forever." In Italy it is still early morning; they have an entire day for sightseeing ahead. They stop and roll a joint, which A.J. lights under the *Rape of the Sabine Women*.

Above their heads, somewhere in the heart of the city, a giant bell is ringing.

The beautiful boy selling his art outside the Uffizi is muscled in a modest way. A.J. has passed by his blanket a dozen times. He hasn't sold a single drawing all afternoon.

"You want one?" he finally says.

Helena has run off with a high school basketball star from the Midwest, someone she found drinking wine on the street, tall and lanky. His name was Roger. He was on a class trip, but said he could steal away if she wanted to see the *Duomo*.

A.J. wanders the city alone. It's early evening. "This one. The heart-shaped pebble."

The beautiful boy laughs: "It's a clove of garlic."

"Oh," A.J. cocks her head. On closer look, he is much older than she is. "How much?"

His T-shirt ripples. "More than you've got."

A.J. sniffs the breeze: "You don't know that."

"Maybe," he smiles. "Where's your friend? The one with the hair?"

A.J. likes that he's noticed them. "She went off with

someone she just met."

The boy frowns. "You don't approve of love?"

"Love?" A.J. is hard-pressed to apply the word to Helena and Roger-from-Cleveland fucking against some ancient crucifix. "More like revenge."

The boy carefully wraps his charcoals in a rag. "This is Florence. Magical things happen."

A.J. is doubtful.

He puts his sketches inside a giant envelope, hesitating before he picks up the one she's chosen. "What's your name?" he asks.

"Alice-James."

"You Americans have weird names." He sticks out his hand. "*Yo soy Pedro de Cuba.*"

A.J. is kissing Pedro from Cuba when an image of her baby brother floats up. She clasps the back of Pedro's neck for more pressure and tries to settle into the pillow, wanting his mouth to blot hers out. *Feel it*, she tells herself, somehow reminded of the numbness of growing up in Pennsylvania. Pedro lifts her shirt and kisses her breasts. She works her hand down his naked back and wonders if she should enter him, where he is not quite wet, but moist—sweaty. This is what keeps a man feeling alive, according to Gordy. A mental picture of Helena laughing relieves her, mercifully, but doesn't stay. Her baby brother leans a head on her shoulder and coos like a little bird. She can recall the squeak of his talcum-y skin, his tiny erections, which sometimes she touched when no one was looking. Then she can hear someone crying; her father, this time with his head on her breast, or maybe the sound comes from her. Pedro sucks her nipples, as if she is a musical instrument on the verge of emitting sweet sounds. She concentrates on maneuvering into an arch to press her finger into his ass.

"Not so fast," Pedro whispers. "Take it easy."

A.J. reminds herself that she is lying naked on a cot in Pedro's studio in Florence. She hears the sounds from *Via Dante Alighieri* below. They are very near the *Duomo*. On their walk to dinner, Pedro had carefully pointed out the site of the great poet's restored medieval home. At the restaurant that seemed like someone's home, he quoted a few lines from the *Inferno* in Italian in a way that seemed only slightly rehearsed. On the walk back to his studio, they had turned corner after corner into plaza after plaza of tourists scouting out ice cream and sidestepping pigeons. The strange world filled A.J. up like a song. She felt alive to be walking in Florence with a stranger, Pedro, who laughed and pointed out sights and called her *niña*.

Now, lying with Pedro, she lights a joint for him and one for herself. This is an offering of love—*maybe not* love, *but something*—because he saved her, because he knows her, because this is her very first time. One joint entirely for him.

"I've never been high before," Pedro says, smiling. "I like it."

"I've never been fucked before." A.J. laughs.

Pedro's features soften. "This is an honor, then."

For a moment, A.J. feels like crying. Pedro puts the marijuana on the windowsill, kissing her gently, placing himself between her legs and entering slowly, touching a chord, something like pain but also like lightness. It is sad suddenly to be so human, A.J. thinks—so merely human. When she opens her eyes, the room swirls. What she recalls is another room from another time. Perhaps this is the essential experience of sex: you remember places from your past, or perhaps they are your future. She doesn't know if her eyes are open or closed, or suddenly who it is, sweaty and gasping, on top of her. She grips the body and pulls it close, hoping for mercy, an end. Pedro finally stops moving, breathing heavily into her neck, then slides slowly out of her body, and they lie still. They share the joint.

Pedro says, "You are no virgin, *mi amor*."

A.J. covers her body with the stale blanket; her breasts seem to spill over onto the bed, her stomach looks fat, her feet too big. She is doughy and pale, enormous in the dark room with the dark man, a stranger, who is about to fall asleep, to leave her there alone.

"That was my first time," A.J. says insistently.

Tears make the room a blur, and she sees now that her life depends on certain difficult half truths. Pedro takes her hand, kissing the knuckles. "Don't listen to me, *niña*. Really. Pedro is foolish."

He squeezes his shoulders into the mattress as he falls asleep, pinning her slightly against the wall.

In the morning, A.J. rushes to meet Helena at the *Piazza Santa Croce* as planned. Jet-lagged and late from oversleeping, A.J. is almost glad that this time it will be Helena waiting on her for a change. Helena is too beautiful for her own good; her teeth are too white, and she's a total liar: *You and me and Florence forever.* Hurrying along, A.J. breaks into a sweat and has to stop to catch her breath. *Too much smoking*, she thinks. Near the Bapistry, the strangest feeling overtakes her, a kind of dizzy sensation that someone is standing on top of the *Campanile*, 276 feet above her head, pointing a rifle at her, slowly pulling her into the cross-hair view and taking aim. She walks more quickly, heads over to the *Ponte Vecchio*, where the sweet-faced Italians will soon be setting up shop. *Love thy brother*, she thinks, sick to her stomach. Tucking her shoulders up near her ears, she shoves her hands deep in her pockets and looks for a place to get a cup of coffee.

The past doesn't matter, A.J. tells herself. *It's the future that counts.*

Outside the cathedral, Helena grills A.J. about Pedro. "Did it hurt?" she wants to know. "Did you like it? The first time always hurts."

It didn't hurt.

"That's weird. It's supposed to hurt." Helena lights a regular cigarette and sits on the step, pulling A.J. down beside her. They are both wearing the same clothes as yesterday, the same clothes they had on in Waynesboro, which now seems like a million miles away. In A.J.'s back pocket is the charcoal drawing folded in half, along with the fifty lira she stole from Pedro, who was still asleep when she slipped out of his apartment.

"What about you?" Maybe in the end, A.J. will escape Waynesboro, too, and travel the world, making everyone she knows part of her past. "How was Roger?"

Helena pulls at the lit cigarette between her lips. "Okay, I guess. Well, actually, Roger was kind of gay. Nothing happened. I went back to the hostel."

If A.J. had spent the night with Helena, she could have avoided the smell of Pedro's body, his small uncomfortable cot, the question he'd left swirling inside her brain.

"Gay?" Her head pounds. "Not another one?"

Helena laughs and sticks out her tongue. "Who asked you?" She jumps up then, and skips up the steps to the cathedral.

Straining to her feet, A.J.'s limbs feel made of stone. "Wait for me." *Miraculous Helena bouncing back*, she thinks, as she trails behind. Not even a hundred brushes with imperfect love can weigh her down.

*

Inside, *Sante Croce* smells of moldy devotion. The great cathedral is dimly lit and packed with old women praying. At the holy water fount, under the enormous vaulted ceiling, Helena stands close behind. A.J. can feel heat radiating off her body and smell the soapy smell of her flesh. Perhaps this is how close Helena stands when she's seducing two-timing Gordy or poor gay Roger from Cleveland.

A.J. looks across the row of pews, longer than a football field, down a separate hallway, where there are statues and paintings as far as the eye can see, elaborate ceramics, Stations of the Cross. At one popular corner, you can put a coin in a slot to light up the Lord, a famous twelfth-century carving. *A mall for the Savior*, A.J. thinks. Through the dark they make their way past the monuments of Michelangelo, Galileo, Machiavelli.

"I need a joint," she says.

"You know what day it is, don't you?"

A.J. thinks it over. "The second day of you and me and Florence forever?"

"Good Friday," Helena corrects. "The day the Jews killed Jesus. My people, your Lord. I hope you're not still mad about that."

A.J.'s laugh breaks the silence, causing a few kneeling women to look up from their prayers. She covers her mouth. "All the more reason I need to smoke."

Helena drags her to the sacristy to light a candle. "Come on," she whispers, pulling A.J. to her knees. "Save our souls."

A.J. rolls her eyes.

"Say a prayer, A.J. You're Catholic. You know, *Forgive me father* and all that jazz."

"I don't know the words."

They settle on their knees before Jesus, who is nailed to his cross. His pinched, mournful face makes A.J. think that maybe he did something to deserve his fate, to be so bound; people don't just go around getting their wounds doused in vinegar for nothing. Son of God or not, he might have done better to keep his mouth shut. But then someone had to die for someone. For everyone.

A.J. herself is nearly free—nearly eighteen—nearly gone. Only her brother and sister will be left behind to talk about how she got out.

Better them in that house than me. Immediately she feels guilty; she never saved anyone, not even herself.

Helena leans forward to ask A.J. to say a prayer for her, but presses her lips to A.J.'s mouth instead. They are warm and dry, her lips, accommodating. A.J. pulls back, but Helena kisses again, tongue lingering lightly on A.J.'s teeth.

"I always wondered." Helena smiles, shrugging. "It's kind of nice."

A.J. blushes and clears her throat, feeling ridiculous.

Helena jabs her with a good-natured elbow. "Oh, don't be stupid, will you? It's no big deal."

An organ begins to play, the notes jumbled. "Meet me outside, A.J. Okay? I'm starving."

A.J. cannot come up with a single prayer: "Thank you." When she looks up at Jesus' sad face, as He stares down at her, offering the hint of a smile.

The light strikes A.J.'s face like fire as she steps out of *San Croce.* The yellow gold is so bright that she has to squint, but she's thankful for the warmth. She's lucky to be alive, lucky that Helena is waiting for her on the bottom step. Waving and grinning, Helena shouts something she doesn't catch because a small crowd of street children appears at the same exact moment, running toward A.J. She smiles, happy to see their grubby faces, their tight balled-up fists, which are raised to Heaven, exultant.

They rush in, their fingers digging into A.J.'s ribs and pockets. This close, she can't tell suddenly whether they are children or tiny dirty women. They stand as tall as her waist and smell of rotten lettuce, hair matted and tangled, clothes made of rags. They squawk like birds, whistle, and smack the air, drawing A.J.'s eye first to the ground, then the sky; to the right and left, until she is dizzy. One of them squeezes her elbow; another throws herself at A.J.'s feet as if for mercy. The human stench is suffocating, the press of knuckles surprisingly warm and forceful.

They seek out A.J.'s softest places.

They touch her everywhere, bruising her skin.

At last they knock her to the ground, covering her completely. Lying prone on the stone steps under the disheveled creatures, A.J. hears Helena call her name. The hands continue to pinch, as if searching for her wallet or her soul. *Not there*, she thinks, relieved to know the truth. When it's over, she will pick herself up and begin again, this time from scratch, with no past at all. Someday, she will not need to wonder if such terrible children mean to love or harm her with their kisses and their small hands of God.

SORRY

MRS.

ROBINSON

MARY-KAY ROBINSON FOLLOWED THE nurse in the blue cardigan.

"Take everything off," the woman said when they arrived at a small room at the end of the hallway. "Underwear too."

At 57, Mary-Kay was hardly unfamiliar with pelvic exams, but she'd recently learned to hold her tongue.

"Thank you," she said.

The other day her daughters had asked what was wrong. "The heart is a cow," she'd said. They just stared at her blankly, though they should have understood: Janet was in the midst of a messy divorce and Lily was dating a construction worker, who was no prize as far as anyone could tell. "Not even the sense to lie down in the pouring rain. Protect the udders."

She'd never figured out exactly how to talk to her girls. All grown up, they seemed ill-prepared for love, probably her fault, though there were other factors: history, difficulty breast-feeding, a near-public affair she'd had years ago with Gerald Howe.

She could still hear her own heart lowing behind the sturdy white fence of her sternum, just above and to the left of a mass she'd found in her abdomen last Wednesday. She'd been lying in bed watching TV with Richard, thumbing through a book. She could have easily rolled over and gone to sleep, but she'd said, "Feel this."

"Shit, Mary-Kay." Richard fingered the lumps. "A pile of rocks."

Mary-Kay carefully removed her clothes, put on the hospital gown, and sat up on the table, inspecting her legs, which were still her finest feature. Her own daughters, flesh of her flesh, had missed the entire point of being female, which was to enflame desire, not drown it out. What if they spent the rest of their lives thinking marriage—that warmish puddle of emotion—was enough?

How could they not?

She'd discovered true passion only by accident, the day she spotted Gerald Howe in his gabardine suit disciplining teenagers down a glossy buffed hallway. There was something sexy about his determination, the certitude of his reprimand. He'd confiscated their marijuana cigarettes, then turned around and waved, saying, "How's my favorite PTA treasure?" In a million years, she wouldn't have figured Gerald Howe, assistant principal at the junior high school, for the man who'd reveal a universe unexplored within her own body.

They shared certain opinions about child rearing. After they both opposed a referendum to close down one of the high schools, other parents began to look to them for guidance: What do Gerald and Mary-Kay think? Soon, Mary-Kay was putting on silk blouses for board meetings, for which she was district treasurer. Once, she rescheduled a hair appointment so her cut would be fresh but not too new.

He kissed her on the lips one evening in the administrator's lounge after a grueling budget negotiation. They were in the middle of putting the coffee urn away. *Darling*, he said, and slowly peeled away her blouse, pressing her into the gray fabric sofa while the other parents got into their cars and drove away.

At climax, he grabbed a fistful of hair, gently at first, then roughly, as if he were exposing her neck to an unseen executioner. No one had ever pulled her hair before. When he wept, out of guilt or passion, she'd felt their destiny like an oncoming train: so random, so inevitable.

That year—1978?—Mary-Kay's youngest daughter, Lily, had been new to the junior high. After an incident involving ninth graders and a Swiss army knife, Mary-Kay started driving her to and from school, taking her out of class an hour early on Tuesdays and Thursdays to steal more time with Gerald. She waved off Gerald's concern about Lily. "Gym class and study hall?" she said. "I think she'll live."

Maybe she'd been rash.

Lily was a serious child, sitting quietly in the back of the family station wagon while Mary-Kay swung around to the side faculty parking lot. "You wait here and do your homework. Okay, honey?" Mary-Kay had headed for the empty bleachers, where Gerald was waiting. "Mommy'll be right back."

Lily never looked up from her books.

Maybe Mary-Kay shouldn't have driven Gerald Howe the few blocks home every afternoon, or convinced Lily over predinner ice cream sundaes that their time alone with Principal Howe was a special secret. Lily never asked a single question; wise beyond her thirteen years, she'd coolly licked fudge from her lips, judging Mary-Kay silently.

After a while, a handsome young man wearing a stethoscope around his neck came sauntering into the examining room where Mary-Kay sat propped on the table.

It was 1997. How had so much time passed by?

He smiled winningly. "Have you been waiting long, Mrs. Robinson?"

"A lifetime," she said.

*

Once, a few years ago, Mary-Kay thought she'd spotted Gerald Howe shelving books at the Barnes & Noble. It was odd she'd never bumped into him before, not once in all the years since he'd politely asked her never to call his house again. He loved his wife; he'd taken a vow.

It wasn't as if they could just go on having an affair.

Mary-Kay hadn't exactly been surprised when he'd called it off; Gerald *had* cried whenever they'd made love. She'd been a fool to think they might continue as they were, forever. Still, she was glad to have had a foolish heart thumping fervently in her chest.

By the time Gerald called it quits, Lily had sailed into high school with honors; Mary-Kay had quit the Westchester PTA, and Richard, poor unsuspecting Richard, was none the wiser. No harm done, except Lily's continued lack of interest in boys and her preoccupation with Mary-Kay, who'd wandered the house at night, stuffing herself with whatever she found in the cabinets, vomiting to get empty. She missed everything there was to miss about Gerald.

"Mom," Lily said, appearing after midnight in her nightgown. "When are you going to stop crying?"

Mary-Kay was hurrying home with Richard's birthday gift when she'd spotted Gerald Howe in the Galleria. It was a Sunday; the girls were coming for pot roast. Maybe Gerald had taken a job in his retirement.

Work keeps the fingers nimble, the mind agile, she imagined him saying.

From across the mall, the sound of his voice came back, the feel of his hands. She sat down on a bench next to a pretzel cart. To think that she might have happened by on any given day of the week and found him there, among the fiction titles! Through the glass, he looked handsome, a little heavier, more gray in his hair. His children had given him grandchildren no doubt; his wife had joined the garden club.

Imagine being so close all this time.

She picked up the Ralph Lauren sweater wrapped and bagged for Richard, and the yellow birthday cake with coconut frosting. She'd come back another day and find him; maybe they'd have a cup of coffee at the food court.

"Hello, Gerald," she whispered. "I've missed your face."

"The name's Douglas, lady," said the kid behind the pretzel cart, handing her a diet coke and some change.

Now Mary-Kay was trying to pay attention to the young doctor in the examining room. There'd been a terrible mistake, a mix-up. The sort of thing that happened to someone else.

The doctor mentioned her ovaries right off the bat.

"I haven't used *that* plumbing in years," she said.

Dr. Green, a man probably in his late thirties and therefore suitable for one of her daughters, was holding her hand. No wedding ring. He continued with the explanation of her diagnosis. Once it had been an ugly old man who'd discussed her fibroids, harmless and dull, nestled like grapefruit in the tree of her womb. Now it was young Dr. Green, with his winsome smile and fancy talk about tumors that metastasize to the liver.

Mary-Kay's mouth was dry. Outside it was still early May.

"There are things you can expect," he said. "Surgery, chemotherapy, radiation."

She studied the peculiar way his hand was lying on top of hers, suggestively covering her bare knuckles, as if he were picking her up in a bar.

Do you do this sort of thing often? she thought, but she was dressed in a paper wrapper. It was not possible to land that kind of joke.

"I need you to be strong, Mrs. Robinson." His formality startled her. Weren't they intimate now? "There's more."

He started speaking about other body parts. Her sphincter had caused some sort of problem, though it didn't seem possible the two were linked—her eroding female organs and that particular portal of elastic tissue. The problem had spread to her skin, Dr. Green explained, or perhaps had started there, or maybe even—there were data to suggest—the two cancers were completely unrelated. A strange coincidence.

"Loosening," he said, "…some grafts to be sure…"

Outside the window, a tree had begun to sprout buds; and beyond that was the parking lot, shiny with windshields. She had the perfect excuse to pick up the phone and dial Gerald Howe now: *Hello, my darling. Good thing you didn't leave your wife after all. Turns out I won't be staying.*

Dr. Green said, "A hysterectomy will be necessary, debulking, a careful protocol of estrogen and progesterone—sometimes itself a risk for cancer."

Mary-Kay's laugh sounded tinny in the little room. "Hysterectomy?"

She'd contracted a disease fitting for someone young with a need for those organs. She'd done her job, used them wisely, birthed and raised her children. She'd found ways to keep busy, managed to forget about passion, to do the honorable thing and leave love alone. She'd even learned to settle into the rest of her life with Richard. Richard! This was out of the question.

"We may be able to save your colon," Dr. Green was saying, "depending on the damage."

She pointed across the room: "Are you sure that's my file?"

He wrote something on the chart.

"My daughters come to this office," she continued, wondering if it sounded suspicious. Involuntarily, she lifted a hand to her bangs. She'd need more highlights now, perhaps a different cut.

"I'm sorry, Mrs. Robinson," Dr. Green said.

Mary-Kay tried one more time: "You don't seem to understand. They're of child-bearing age; they still use these parts." When Richard felt the mass in her abdomen, he'd suggested they call an ambulance. She wanted to tell the doctor: Couldn't he just imagine ever-practical Richard picking up the phone for 911?

Dr. Green looked at her expectantly. He held his pen, poised, over a future sentence. What could he be writing? A report on her behavior? *Mary-Kay Robinson tried to bargain for her life. She implicated the innocent.*

Maybe he just wanted to let go of her hand.

More than anything Mary-Kay wished she could be somewhere else, or not anywhere. *The waiting room:* limbo, a no man's land where she could still pretend to know herself, be free from thinking the very next thought. She wanted to be patiently or nervously pacing, while someone else, anyone else—one of her daughters—sat in a white paper dress with the young doctor and took it like a man.

She was an awful person. And that was why.

"It takes time to sink in," Dr. Green said, kindly. "I'm very sorry."

"Not you! You shouldn't be sorry. It's me." She was certain he could see right through her. "I'm the one."

Not them, not my daughters.

She saw herself clearly: all the pain and sorrow and stolen hearts, all the diaper pins and menstrual pads and parent-teacher conferences. Had they all been for nothing?

The point was *the nonsense and minutiae,* Gerald might say. *All of it just insane enough to make each kiss indelible.* She began to cry at the thought of his voice.

The very possibility, an oasis.

PRETEND
I'M YOUR
FRIEND

PRETEND I'M YOUR FRIEND

SITTING IN HER APARTMENT with two police officers, Marie is stunned, not because her boyfriend, David, killed himself in the bathroom, but because it is April and 1999, a year to party, if you believe the song by Prince.

"Open and shut," the taller cop says.

Marie never realized before that people could die in warm weather.

"Nothing suspicious here," says the second cop.

"My baby brother fell through a frozen pond once and drowned," she tells the police, who peel tape off the doorjamb and gather up their note pads. "My uncle died in a blizzard. Of course, that was in the seventies. Weather has changed."

Outside on the front stoop, where the air is gentle, the policemen squint sadly and shake Marie's hand. Over their shoulders, Marie spots Susan coming up the block, carrying a pot of her famous yogurt-spinach soup. As the squad car pulls out into the street, Marie realizes that she could just shut her door and lock it. *This is your best friend*, she reminds herself. Susan turns up the path, face blotchy with grief.

"I would have been nicer to David," Susan says, "but he was such a drug addict."

They stand on the front stoop, looking at one another, as if someone else might open the door and let them in. *My apartment,* Marie reminds herself, motioning Susan into the foyer.

It's almost lunchtime. They decide to eat the soup, though there is cleaning to do. Four friends from high school are due to arrive this evening to cheer and comfort Marie during her crisis. Susan has made arrangements.

At the table, Marie watches her line up the salt and pepper shakers, the napkins, and the water glasses, all in an even row. "Are you sure he didn't leave a note, Marie? Did you check his pockets?"

Chopped eggs float in the soup like pulverized rubber balls: yellow and green. "No note."

"I suppose you'll wait to date," Susan says. "I mean, I suppose you'll stay with men and all, right? It's got to be easier with men."

Marie looks hard at Susan's round face. Now that David is gone, all her friends will start to worry about alternative attractions. "A little early to tell."

Susan looks down at her soup. "Sorry."

In the mirror, Marie practices telling her friends, who are due to arrive this afternoon. "Actually, I'm already seeing someone."

The words seem unconvincing.

"Olive," Marie says, trying to believe it herself.

As if her expressions were governed by the tight barrette holding back her hair, Olive barely moved her face when she first smiled at Marie. She showed up with the crisp fall air, a new junior lawyer on the floor, ambitious and chatty, which Marie could see the senior lawyers considered a liability. Silently they suffered her cheerful greetings: "Hello! Hi there! Look at you!

What a day!" Passing by each plush office, she stuck her pointy face into the doorway and spoke loudly.

"She just wants attention," said one of the other data processors.

Marie could hear the partners scratching their pens onto legal pads. She'd been temping the night shift since November: a hundred pre-formatted files, printed and stapled to a hundred long sheets of blue construction paper. *Blue backs* the secretaries called them.

Olive always found her way to the data station where Marie and the others were assembled for nightshift in a temporary horseshoe of computers. She immediately started talking to Marie, the only woman, the only non-actor, non-artist, non-poet in the crew. The only one without a true purpose. Marie was lost, a state she could never seem to hide or shake.

"Attorney is my day job," Olive said confidentially. "But I'm a writer, too."

Marie stared at Olive's Armani blazer.

"I mean, I *have* to write," Olive continued. She took a seat on the edge of Marie's desk, which everyone in the office referred to as data-entry station #1. "It's like a religion with me."

"What do you write?" Marie said.

"Oh, everything. Plays, novels. Whatever."

Mostly, Marie knew, Olive wrote steamy little lists she sent out electronically:

PRETEND I MET YOU IN AN ELEVATOR.

PRETEND YOU ARE A BAD GIRL.

PRETEND YOU KNOW ALL MY SECRETS.

PRETEND I DON'T WORK DOWN THE HALL.

"What about you?" Olive asked.

"Oh I don't write anything." Marie said, hoping this explained the fact that she never returned Olive's e-mailed love notes, or her cyber advances. "Bad checks, sometimes."

"No, I mean generally." Olive laughed. "Where are you from?"

"Cleveland, I guess," Marie said. "We moved around a lot. I was born in Rome."

"Sounds exotic!"

"Rome, New York," Marie said. "It's Upstate."

Olive scratched her head with the eraser end of a pencil. "You look Jewish."

"Italian." Marie's hands were still poised above the keyboard, ready to finish typing her assignment. It was getting late.

Olive pressed her nose to the side, mugging a scowl: "Mafia?"

"Insulting," Marie said, but smiled. Olive *was* technically her boss.

"Just kidding," Olive said.

In Cleveland, in the early 80s, Marie's father had worked overtime to provide for his family. A carpet contractor, he had aimed for a low profile, while impeccably furnishing certain important offices downtown for certain important people. For most of her adolescence, Marie had had no idea that her best friend Gina was the great grandniece of one of the most important mobsters alive, Reni Piscaretti. Once, she'd overheard her parents fighting the morning after a dinner party with the Piscarettis, at the Blue Rose Restaurant, later site of the famous slayings.

He asked me, Carlo. Marie's mother's voice trembled. *He pointed it in my face and said, Come on, taste! What was I supposed to say?*

Her father was furious: *Guys lined up for miles to poison that S.O.B., and you eat off his fork? Smart, Celine, real smart.*

That afternoon, her mother took a cab to the hospital to have her collarbone set, as her father tended to overemphasize his point with a punch or slap. He was a violent man, but only after drinking too much.

At the periphery of Marie's desk, Olive's foot wiggled in an expensive pump. "You married?"

"Married?" Marie repeated.

"Yeah, you know, *with* somebody?"

"David," Marie said. "We live together."

"David?" Olive paused. "I was expecting something more feminine. Dana, maybe. Daveen."

Marie let her fingers fall in their proper position over the keys: "Not this time."

Olive didn't answer.

Marie hated silence and added a few words to lighten things up. "But thanks for asking."

The cat jumps up on the kitchen table, startling Susan, who spills her soup.

Marie's been thinking of changing the cat's name. "What about Heathcliff?"

"I don't like it." Susan wipes the table with her napkin. "How about Honey?"

With David, Marie got to make most of the decisions. He didn't care about things, as long as she was happy. She'll miss that. She is sad to be thrust back into a world of negotiating with other people.

"Anyway, I think she's in heat," Susan says, watching the cat howl and hunch.

After they took David's body away, Marie cleaned for hours, using paper towels and garbage bags. There was even blood matted into the cat's fur.

After the initial shock, she tried calling Olive at home, but Jewel, Olive's girlfriend, answered the phone. She explained her situation into Olive's voicemail at work, asking for a temporary leave of absence. Human Resources called back, and later in the week, the legal secretaries sent flowers with a note card offering condolences from Dean, Dean, & Dean. For a few days Marie waited for Olive to call her, but the week since David's suicide passed in silence. For some reason, she imagined the message Olive might have sent out electronically at work:

BLEW HIS BRAINS OUT IN BATHROOM!

HIGH AS KITE.

CAT WAS ONLY WITNESS.

"Maybe in college you had sex with women as a reaction to your childhood," Susan says, starting to clear the soup bowls. "Violence will do that to a person."

Marie doesn't know how to tell Susan that her childhood is why she has sex with *men*; she's striving for mastery. Sex with women is what feels good.

She can't seem to bring up Olive.

"It's hard to explain," Marie says.

After the first time Marie and Olive made love on top of a desk in a dark law office—quite by accident and never again, Marie vowed almost immediately—Marie worried that David would figure it out. She started arriving home from work even later than usual, collapsing in bed unwashed. David nudged his head under her arm, pressing against her. His body, thin and ropy with muscle, made her feel even more pudgy than usual.

He leaned on his elbows, trying to kiss her.

"It's late," Marie said.

David spoke in a low voice into the pillow: "The late great David Schenkel."

"Are you high again?"

He rolled onto his back. "No."

"Did you go to class tonight?"

With his head pulled back on the pillow, it would have been easy to crush his windpipe.

"Yes, I went," he mumbled, pulling her close. "You smell good."

"Aren't you sleepy?" Marie whispered, smoothing his hair.

He pressed her hands against his nostrils, inhaling a trace of Olive's scent. "Seriously, Babe, what's that smell?"

"It's nothing. Go back to sleep."

Night after night in a dark office, it was the same. The entire sexual act taking less than twenty minutes: a sentence without adjectives, a verb, followed by another verb, two nouns in a tangle. They never bothered to undress completely, taking turns going down on each other; first Marie, then Olive.

"Be yourself," Olive whispered.

Marie could always see a trace of light down the hall, partners working late. The directive was confusing. *Myself?* Marie considered it.

In bed at home, she closed her eyes and leaned close to David, her stomach fluttering with secrets.

With Olive, at least, despair was a sentence she could imagine:

I'M TIRED OF PRETENDING.

．

After four months on the nightshift data-entry legal team, sleeping till noon, heading into Manhattan when everyone was leaving, Marie thought about doing something important with her life: the LSATs, the Peace Corps, working in AIDS. She missed camaraderie; she missed sunshine.

One day, on her way to work at the beginning of the shift, rising to the 40th floor, Marie shared an elevator with Olive, who was holding a deli sandwich. "Can you believe this is lunch?"

"Busy day," Marie said, as if they were strangers. It had to be at least six p.m.

Olive lit a cigarette under a no smoking sign, exhaling dramatically. "Don't believe everything you read, Miss Thing."

The other data entry workers were generally cold to Marie, East-Village types in the arts. They arrived in chatty clusters with bags of junk food. They recounted episodes of television shows Marie had never seen. They discussed city politics. Behind her back, they referred to her as *Data Bitch*.

"You guys couldn't make it in this office in broad daylight," she told one of them once after they'd made fun of her perfect stack of finalized blue backs.

The stupid one laughed, and the other guy gave Marie the finger and threw a crumpled bag of Doritos at her computer screen.

At nine p.m., alone in the tiny kitchen, during her dinner break, Marie watched darkness descend. Pinpricks of light came up over Manhattan one by one. Despite a warning posted next to the refrigerator—*It is not safe to unseal these panes*—she opened the window. Later, Olive sent an e-mail:

YOU BETTER BE CAREFUL TO HEED ALL SIGNS.

ON THE 40TH FLOOR, YOU CAN GET SUCKED OUT.

When Marie refused to respond, Olive sent a status report.

ROGERS V. ROGERS DUE MONDAY A.M.
CLIENT MEETING. LET ME KNOW YOUR E.T.A—A.S.A.P.
GIRLFRIEND OUT OF TOWN TILL TUES.
SHE (JEWEL) AND I HAVE BEEN TOGETHER TWO YEARS
(LESBIAN FOREVER). THIS ENTITLES ME TO DO
WHAT I WANT.
LET ME KNOW YOUR SCHED.

Marie dragged the icon of the message to the trash at the bottom of her screen, knowing that when everyone left, she would succumb to Olive in one of the empty offices.

No reply was necessary.

At midnight sharp, when the data boys disappeared, leaving Marie to clean up the mess—pizza boxes, bags of chips, half-finished legal briefs, cans of soda, stains on the rug—Olive came up behind her.

"What are you, the cleaning staff?" she asked.

After lunch, Susan dusts the living room with a washcloth and pops open a beer. The way she flips the top with her thumb and forefinger reminds Marie of the little pistol David carried in his waistband and used variously as a bottle opener, doorstop, and paperweight. He was always pulling it out and banging it around to make himself feel handy. Marie puts down her mop and stretches in the salmon-colored armchair by the table, which David once dragged to the kitchen so he could eat, watch TV, shoot up, and doze in comfort at the same time. She looks through the rear window at the fenced-in concrete square passing as a Brooklyn garden. Last spring, David planted a little row of marijuana along the fence in their garden with some tulips. This spring, they bloomed before he killed himself. There won't be a funeral service of any type; his mother wants the body sent back home. Lately, Marie notices, the cat no longer seems to feel like chasing birds.

"A nap?" Marie says, seeking permission.

Susan holds up a box of hair color, Dark Ash Blonde. Her honeyed roots and dark eyes match the leopard-skin leotard she wears under her overalls. Susan, three or four inches taller than a child, wants to look fresh and alive when the others arrive. David used to call her *Shorty*.

"You nap," she says. "I'll dye."

The cat rubs its scent along the perimeter of the wallpaper, prowling and crouching as it goes, stopping only once to gag and then vomit.

For most of the affair, Olive was loose and beautiful, her long legs meeting in the middle, hungry and wet. When Marie put her hand inside Olive, she felt the danger of being swallowed up whole. Though what really could happen? Olive's e-mails demonstrated she was too self-absorbed to be threatening:

> PRETEND THE WORLD IS AT YOUR DISPOSAL.
>
> HAVE MORE AMBITION: BECOME A PARALEGAL.

Marie used to arrive home from work exhausted after David was asleep. She'd feed the cat half a can of turkey giblets from the fridge.

"Eat up," she told David's cat, one of his many strays. Young men, cats, and people's mothers were always David's specialty. Usually he was responsible for getting them hooked, so he could save them by cutting them off. One grandmother type still leaves fresh-baked cookies on the front stoop in gratitude.

"People need to be surrounded by life," David said whenever a new stray arrived. He put them up in the guest room. "It reminds us we're tribal at heart."

Comments like these were supposed to make it okay when the mailman, for instance, nodded out on the sofa, or the next-door neighbor concocted God-Knows-What in the kitchen to sell to kids in the schoolyard.

Marie had always liked the animal strays best.

"We're not cats, Marie," David said with the latest one, happily scrubbing a pregnant feline in the bathroom. "That's important information."

He studied the whiskers, the tail and pink padding under the cat's feet. "I'm calling this new one Horsy."

"Please, no," Marie said. "No drug names."

"For old times' sake, Babe," David said. "Besides I quit today. For good. Had it."

Marie nodded, as if she hadn't heard it a hundred times. "That's great."

"Great?" David lifted the cat onto a clean towel. "I'm a failed drug pusher! What's so great about that?"

Eventually Marie started to devise new ways out of her cycle of lying and sneaking. "Wake up, David," she whispered, hovering over him in a bathrobe.

"What?" Under David's dirty pajamas and narrow chest, he was pure heartache.

She brought a belt down hard across his ankles. "You left your clothes on the hall floor."

"It won't happen again." His voice was breathy.

"No, it won't," Marie said. "Take your pajamas off."

He was quivering.

"You're not allowed to come, this time, David. Do you hear me?"

"Yes, Ma'am," he said, excited already.

They had not had sex in months, and Marie was relieved by the familiarity, the push and pull of it, the being in charge, excitement rising between them.

"I love you, David," Marie said.

As he moaned in the dark, she beat him into orgasm.

Now, Marie naps in the back bedroom. She wakes to the cat kneading her with its paws, then hears Susan answer the door, greeting their friends.

Gina Piscaretti speaks in a low voice.

She can hear Susan answer: "Depressed…lot of sleeping… bisexual again…extra touchy." When Gina's Great Uncle Reni was slain at the Blue Rose, Marie's mother said she'd never met a kinder man in all her life.

"Bisexual?" she hears Gina say.

Everyone laughs.

Marie remembers how once she dutifully cleaned up David's diarrhea as he lay trying to get clean on the futon she's currently sprawled across. The cat makes a comforting paperweight on her chest. Marie scratches its ears, nuzzling closer.

From where they are curled around each other—half-asleep, half-awake—Marie can see the darkening sky, the last rays of orange sun. April is almost gone. She listens to her childhood girlfriends giggling in the kitchen, drinking beer, setting the table, gossiping.

Words from a recent Olive e-mail float into Marie's head:

LET'S BE CASUAL, NOT COMPLICATED.
I'M IN IT FOR FUN. HOW ABOUT YOU?
TELL ME YOUR SECRETS.
PRETEND I'M YOUR FRIEND.

There's a knock on the door.

"Everyone's here," Susan says gently.

Marie's limbs are like stone. "Be right out."

She gets up, putting David's cat into a duffel bag, leaving the zipper open a bit for breathing room. She finds some clothes and puts them in her backpack.

Leaning a folding chair to the window, she climbs out as quietly as she can.

Tip-toeing to the front stoop, she unlocks her bike. The bare light glows through her front window: Her old friends are laughing in there, putting their arms around one another, raising their bottles in a glinting circle of amber-colored glass, reunited after many years. Marie listens for the happy sound of clinking beer.

She likes the idea of spying on her life through shabby curtains, finding happiness there.

Outside, it's getting chilly. On her bike, Marie makes her way along the empty streets to the railroad tracks across town. The cat bounces against the handlebars as her bike's thin tires hit the tracks. They remind her of the bruised veins in David's ropy arms.

She pedals and holds on.

*

On the first train waiting at Atlantic Avenue, she takes a seat near the door, across from a sleeping woman, whose clothes and glasses remind her of Olive. At this moment, the real Olive might be sending her an e-mail:

IT'S NOT OKAY FOR PEOPLE TO JUST DISAPPEAR.

Once the train starts moving, Marie unzips the bag, letting the cat's head stick out.

"Cute," the sleeping woman says, apparently only resting her eyes for show. "What's her name?"

"Oh, it's Honey, I guess."

"Nice." The woman has the same ironic intonation as Olive. Even so she is pretty.

"Someone else named her," Marie says.

"Where are you going?" the woman asks.

Nowhere, thinks Marie. They sway with the motion of the train.

"Penn Station."

"And after that?"

"Somewhere warm," Marie says. "What about you?"

"I'm leaving too." The woman tugs at the red scarf tied around her neck. "Things didn't work out so well here."

The cat begins to make more noise. The woman scratches its ears.

"I used to have cats." She looks at Marie. "Before...well... whatever."

Marie pushes the cat's head back in the bag.

"Things never got right," the woman adds. "What else can a person do?"

This is more information than Marie bargained for. Still, the woman looks so sad Marie can't judge her harshly.

As more people board the train, the woman slides into the seat next to Marie. She places her cashmere coat on her knees to cover the cat as people make their way down the aisle.

In the dark glass of the train's dirty window, they are a pair already: Marie in the foreground looking young and lost; the well-dressed woman next to her sleepy and worn.

The cat twitches.

Marie wonders if the cat ever dreams about what happened in the bathroom: David pounding open the bathroom window with his little pearly gun, not even high, just stupid; the sound of something loud and searing, the smell of something sweet and dripping. The cat, warm and wet, growing very still, feeling sick, vomits up a hairball when it senses that death has come. One or two thuds and then nothing, nothing, nothing.

For a long time, nothing.

On the train, the cat twitches, purrs, and yawns. Marie puts her hand in the bag for the warmth of another living being. *We're not cats, Marie.* They pass stops where Marie could get off and get back home easily if she wanted. Soon, on another train, they will pass houses and fields and ponds that look exactly like the spot where her brother Sal drowned and her uncle froze to death one very unlucky winter.

Marie closes her eyes.

Under the soft coat the woman pets David's cat, rubbing under its chin, listening to the steady sound of purring.

"There, there, Honey," she says.

PEOPLE
SAY
THANK YOU

VIOLET'S PSYCHIC VISION ABOUT her sister came on a Thursday. It was a few moments before the blue-plate special arrived—no croutons, dressing on the side—near the end of the millennium.

"I have information to suggest you're in for trouble," Violet said, putting her cell phone down on the table and settling in for what promised to be a stormy meal. "It's the nanny, I think. My suggestion is to fire her."

Sometimes the onset of the precognitions came as a strange sensation in her body, just under the skin: not quite a headache, not quite a shiver. Like edging toward something, like sifting through junk mail in the mind. Then—like now— there came a splintering open, a warm wash of light, through which undeniably valuable information emerged.

Judith blinked back a few tears, reaching for her glass of water. "Where do you come up with this stuff?"

"I'm telling you, it's bad. Maybe Ray's been a decent husband, but there *are* things you need to know."

Often Violet felt as if she were channeling someone else, though when she looked down at her own white blouse and floral skirt, her own fashionable patent-leather sandals, she saw it was only herself. The experience was strange yet familiar. Since childhood, she had nurtured these talents, making not necessarily big predictions about The Future, but intuiting smaller difficulties that might easily be avoided with grace.

Nothing wrong with a little advance warning. People either listened or they didn't.

Violet remained cautious, especially around her family, weighing the good against the bruising and scarring that might result when she opened her mouth.

Judith shook her head.

"Nannies don't generally show up at four in the morning, do they?" Violet whispered. "They don't instinctively know when Ray's having insomnia, or when the light in his study might be on. That kind of knowledge requires driving around in the family Suburban at God-knows-what hour. Prowling without headlights. Don't tell me Ray hasn't encouraged it."

Violet pointed to her cell phone lying next to the butter.

"I can't just call her mother," Judith said. "Nothing has happened. And besides, they're neighbors, Vi. The last thing we need is more talk about Ray. I'll never find another babysitter."

Violet felt a momentary blur behind her eyes, as if a bare lightbulb had been switched on. Words ran through her mind like ink—indelible—and she knew it as surely as she was sitting in a restaurant with Judith: the deed was as good as done. The present was still the present, she reminded herself: This was her little sister. This was her brother-in-law, of whom she'd always suspected something.

"He's doing it, Judy."

Judith blew her nose on the wad of Kleenex crumpled in her fist. "I don't understand you, Violet. These ridiculous pronouncements of yours."

The salads arrived. "Call the girl's mother," Violet said. "It's one simple sentence: *Your child's services are no longer required.* Then hang up."

"This is a story about how I didn't get much sleep last night because of a hang-up caller, not some sordid porno movie about the babysitter!"

"Then why are you crying?"

A waiter appeared holding a pepper mill under Violet's nose; she motioned him away.

"I never did believe Ray's story about the you-know-what," she thought aloud.

Judith's face turned red. "Ancient history? Is that what this is about?"

Most of the people who took Violet seriously were initially stunned, sat there like sheep that she'd dragged to slaughter, but by the end of her vision—through which Violet usually stumbled like an idiot savant reciting Lear—they acted relieved. *Lightning strikes, and people say thank you.*

Judith shifted in her chair, dipped a carrot into her dressing.

Her sister wasn't the same girl she'd once been, Violet thought; she used to be a fighter. Violet reached across the table and patted Judith's hand. It was a family trait to ignore good sense, however it arrived.

Once Violet delivered the information, she was done. Her body returned to its normal, dull existence; her mind settled down. She ate lettuce and carried on conversations like everyone else. Whatever happened with the information after that was merely the natural fulfillment of things to come.

That Monday Judith caught Ray in the pantry, the girl's jeans unbuttoned, shirt pulled up. A series of phone calls, a violent shoving match (inadvertently involving eight-year-old Ray Jr.), and a brief stay at Motel Six followed. Then, tenuously, the first quivers of reconciliation. Ray got on his knees and made promises.

In exchange for her silence, the nanny was given a severance package.

"Violet," Judith said without anger, gratitude, or a trace of relief, "you fucking amaze me."

Edward Fields, minor Mid-Atlantic poet of fleeting renown and Violet's husband of twenty years, was more exuberant about her gifts. "The truth, Violet! The absolute truth! You've helped me find my way."

They'd been bickering for several weeks about the unkempt lawn. Edward was interested in art, not obligation.

Then came the light and a location, a Southern state.

"Oh, go to Georgia!" Violet had said inexplicably in the middle of their next fight about salting the icy front walkway. As happened so often, the words popped out of her mouth without warning, their meaning unknown to her.

"Do you know what a remarkable thing this is?" Edward was still holding her hand. "After all these years? To think you are the one to offer me happiness so generously. But of course it would be you. Who else? Extrasensory Violet!"

Violet wanted to take it back. "I didn't mean it literally."

"But therein lies the brilliance," Edward said. After all these years, he said he no longer loved her; perhaps he never had. "I'm lazy. I need someone to take control, someone who will do it all for me. That's where Georgia comes in."

Georgia McFeely was a fifty-three-year-old rare-books librarian, and Edward's lover, apparently. Violet had met her once briefly at a Rutgers faculty party.

"You're in love with her?" Violet said, slowly catching on. She felt her stomach rotate.

"Georgia wants a lazy lover." Edward was never one to spare the gritty details. "I swear, Violet. All she wants me to *do* is lie back. She even binds my hands and feet. It's absolutely fantastic! And you understand! You have given me permission through your divination. It's perfect! A gift from God!"

He grinned at her from across the sofa. In all likelihood he was leaving, he said.

A slave state, Violet thought.

"I thought you'd be happy," Edward said. "You know, given how dissatisfied you've been."

He was right. She should have seen it coming.

Violet could pinpoint the exact moment things had gone awry. She'd been helping her mother settle into a new room at the nursing home in Plainsboro. After a difficult morning of name-calling and wrist holding—twice Violet's mother had mistaken her for someone else and twice called her a cunt—Violet had offered to shampoo her mother's hair.

Surprisingly, her mother seemed delighted by the idea.

Violet placed two folding chairs one behind the other on the sun porch so she could take the tangles out of her mother's hair as they watched the sun setting across Route 103.

It was a lovely moment.

Violet felt calm—even affectionate—as she slowly unpinned her mother's bun, untwisted the long braid, and began caressing a length of silver in her hand. *Like ribbon*, she thought.

Her mother hummed.

The sun sank in a slow glinting arc over New Jersey, until it was nothing more than a glowing memory. In the dim room, her mother began to speak lucidly.

"Violet," she said, "I've been thinking about your life."

"Really? What have you been thinking?"

"I've been thinking that you need a little more life in it."

Violet was touched, as if her mother actually wished the best for her. "That's probably true."

"All those papers you grade," she said. "All that time with

Edward and his insipid poetry."

"Now, Mother."

"No, really, Violet." Her mother straightened in her chair. Her voice became urgent. "How do you expect me to keep track of who you are when you don't even know yourself?"

Violet opened her mouth.

"Look at you!" her mother said to her reflection in the dark window. "When's the last time Violet Stern Fields had a good laugh? Does she *ever* laugh? And when's the last time Violet Stern Fields had a good time?" Each question felt like a slap. Her mother turned in the chair to face her. "I mean, Violet, have you *ever* had an orgasm?"

Violet saw herself in the windowpane: a shock of curly hair, a gash of mouth. Tears blurred her vision.

Violet's mother yanked the brush from her hand and said in a completely different voice, "What say we stir up some trouble in the TV lounge?"

After a long, teary drive home, Violet found Edward in the study grading papers and insisted they make love there and then on the oak desk.

After, she'd said, "We're going to start making love every week. And with a little vigor, if you don't mind."

Edward murmured and went back to his work.

She'd actually grabbed his shoulders. "Do you know any good jokes, Edward? Can you please make me laugh?"

Now here he was, holding her hand and pinning his midlife crisis on her. "Be happy for me and Georgia. We found each other. Be happy for someone."

Violet stood up and left the dining room. The house seemed absurdly dark. She stood in the hallway for a long time, waiting to figure out where exactly she could go.

I should cut up his clothes. I should scratch the walls.

Eventually she lay down on the bed in the guest room, hearing Edward whisper and giggle into the phone, listening for her own name.

But she couldn't make out any words.

For the next few months Violet noted Edward's early morning disappearances and absent evenings—once he didn't come home until nearly dawn. During his hushed phone conversations in other rooms or repeated trips to the mailbox, Violet graded papers, wrote student recommendations, and developed academic proposals for Montclair Community College. She was an adjunct, earning little except a bit of respect for her commitment and hard work. Edward composed poetry, drank red wine with his colleagues, conducted workshops for eager budding souls, mostly freshmen at Rutgers, whom he had over for parties in their living room. Violet came to think of their life as boot camp, a kind of kamikaze training of the heart.

If I can withstand this, I can withstand anything.

The new realizations came to her slowly. She'd line-edited hundreds of his poems, and yet he'd never once in all the years offered to read her scholarship on pedagogy. His adamant views on the Middle East and the direction of toilet paper rolls were no more valid than her own opinions about how the world worked.

It got to be that the thought of Edward in his pajamas, flossing his teeth, brushing thoroughly, then flossing again, made Violet's skin go cold. She'd borne witness to this ritual morning and evening for twenty-two years. What did she have to show for it?

Edward hadn't wanted children, so they'd had none. He suddenly stopped wanting commitment, so now they were divorcing.

Maybe it was as simple as it seemed: She'd found a way to stop loving him too.

This new situation reminded Violet of a former colleague, a temperamental Spanish history specialist named Marjorie Dennis. Violet could still conjure the woman's ripe perfume and beautiful silk blouses, each with a coffee stain prominently visible.

A tall, bony woman with large blond waves that threatened to swallow her head, she had nervously appeared last fall in Violet's doorway with a stack of student papers. "Someone else is going to have to grade these."

Violet tried to size up the damage. "You have at least fifty papers there."

Marjorie hugged the curling pages: "Three months' worth."

"You haven't graded a single paper since September?"

"Nothing's really wrong," Marjorie said. "But everything is wrong, you know?"

Violet felt the light descend through the ceiling of the MCC language building and through the top of her head.

"I don't know what's the matter with me, Violet. If only I could explain."

Violet smiled sadly. "Dare I suggest that you simply hate the smell of ink?"

The semester was nearly done; the price of liberating someone from herself meant Violet's workload would double.

"*Ink*." Marjorie hugged Violet briefly. "That's it!"

Violet marked the extra student assignments on her lunch break and on weekends, picking up the abandoned class using Marjorie's syllabus. She skimmed the textbooks and lectured from old notes.

"Professor Dennis has taken a leave," she told the students.

Violet would hatch her own escape, as soon as the last red letter grade was dry. She would leave New Jersey, state of her birth.

"Georgia can have you," she told Edward at dinner. "I'm through with this part of my life."

Right there at the dinner table came a strange new sensation. *Freedom*, Violet thought.

The "No Nukes" button hanging on the bulletin board over Jack Flannery's perfectly shaped bald head made Violet wonder if she'd stumbled into some sort of hippie den.

"Welcome to Flannery Travel," he said. "We aim to get you out of town as fast as you please."

Violet laughed. "Fast is my goal."

Flannery had a marvelous face, small and tightly drawn, with sparkling blue eyes to make a person feel warm and focused. He wore preppie clothes and had a squarish, nicely formed body, perhaps from weekend jogging, Violet thought. His smile was noncommittal, but genuine.

"Summer in Europe," he echoed her request, "a very nice choice, if you don't mind my saying."

Violet felt relief, as if he'd been there all along waiting to help at this precise moment. "I want to go the moment school is out."

"I might have taken you for a teacher," said Flannery tentatively. "You're so well-spoken."

"College," she said.

His manicured fingers tapped the keyboard efficiently as he talked about bookings, hotels, and bus tours. Violet studied his face while they waited for affordable fares to emerge on the screen.

"All this fuss over Y2K ruining our computers will probably come to nothing," he said. He seemed so nice, she considered telling him about her situation. "Packaged tours in European countries are quite special."

She'd only mentioned Georgia to Judith, who'd grown bitter from her own recent experience. Hard to believe: the two Stern girls, middle-aged and disappointed in love.

Jack Flannery regarded her with kind eyes that made him seem a bit too interested, needy maybe, Violet thought.

"I think Alta Vista Bus Tours will be just the thing for you, Mrs. Fields."

She pressed her chest to the top corner of his gray metal desk. It was cold.

"Violet Fields," he added. "What a lovely name."

"It's Stern," she said abruptly. "I'm taking back my maiden name, and there's nothing lovely about that."

Flannery drew back. "I didn't mean anything by it, I..."

The heat rushed to Violet's cheeks. She looked toward the mall's sparse crowd.

"I'd like to be gone Memorial Day until Labor Day, please."

He typed a few more words onto the keyboard, then set his printer to printing.

Violet was silent until he handed her a kit, everything she would need to disappear.

"Thank you, Mr. Flannery," she said.

When Violet pulled out of the mall's dark parking lot, most of the customers had already gone home. Backing the car out, she caught herself in the rearview mirror as if for the first time.

She pointed the car toward the curb in front of the Walmart exit, a last-ditch effort to make herself clear. Her excitement turning to panic, she left the engine running and walked back to Flannery's Travel.

The doors were locked.

"Mr. Flannery," Violet called, knocking loudly on the glass until a security guard emerged from the dark. "Jack?"

"Flannery's gone for the night." The guard adjusted his uniform, feeling for his flashlight.

"But I need to speak to him," Violet said, absurdly. "I've made a terrible mistake."

The guard shrugged, then glanced over the few remaining parked cars in the lot and pointed past where Violet's car sat puffing out white smoke, to a center aisle. "There he is. Row J7, maroon car. If you run, you can catch him."

Violet tapped his shoulder, startling him. "Thank you very much."

She ran in skirt and heels. "Mr. Flannery, wait!"

He turned, key in the door, his L.L. Bean parka too much for the unusually mild night. "Ms. Stern," he said, surprised.

"Please," she was out of breath, "Violet."

"I can't seem to get that right, can I?" He smiled.

"It's me," she said. "I'm really very sorry."

He held his hand up. "No need to apologize."

"I was rude."

"Just a little stressed, I imagine. Most of my customers are."

Slightly stung by the comparison, she stood next to his Buick Century, running her hand along his windshield. She hugged herself then, feeling a tingle in her jaw. "I have something else to say."

Jack Flannery leaned awkwardly on the car's hood. "I'm all ears."

"What was it again?" she said, laughing, embarrassed, concentrating on her headache.

"Change your mind about leaving?"

"No, not that."

She'd moved into the guest bedroom permanently, she wanted to say. At first she couldn't sleep all by herself that way, the first time in decades. Yet lying awake, she'd rediscovered the secret thrills of her body—thrills far better than sleeping with her husband. She wanted to tell Jack Flannery about the intensity of her orgasms. There was no vision, no warm wash of light, no forecast for the future; just a man and a woman standing in a parking lot.

"I'm afraid of what comes next," Violet said finally. She watched his posture soften, wondering if she should have used his name. *Jack.*

The final lamplights went off above their heads, and the Walmart at the end of the complex went black.

"Next is a great vacation," Jack Flannery said. They could barely see each other now. "And after that, you play it by ear—like the rest of us do."

He took a step closer in the dark, reaching for her. "Where'd you go?" he said, holding her by the coat lapel.

The light from her skin was glowing. As her lips touched his, a million phosphorescent particles rose up, shimmering against the black night. She was only human, like everyone else, a woman, heartbroken and recovering.

She pulled Jack Flannery closer, as if she might otherwise evaporate; as if she needed simply a stranger who'd been kind, simply this.

"Amazing," he said, as Violet lit up the dark.

ALICE JAMES'S
CUBAN GARLIC

ALICE-JAMES'S CUBAN GARLIC

I'M STANDING IN THE kitchen with Ma and Alice-James, talking about the plan.

"You kidding me?" Ma says. She shakes her head as if Bo weren't lying just upstairs in the bed Alice-James borrowed from the county hospital. "I don't know what's gotten into you two."

Ma exhales a stream of cigarette smoke, which hangs momentarily on her lip before curling into the predawn air.

"I don't see why not," says Alice-James. "It's his body."

Ma shoots her a look while I pour the coffee, reminding myself silently that it's my kitchen, my coffee, my husband Bo. He got sick in 1997, Year of The Ox, according to the Chinese calendar, a year of health, but not for us.

Ma lights another cigarette. "C'mon, will you?"

"Well, why shouldn't Bo go to the waddayacallit ceremony?" Alice-James says. "Commitment."

Ma groans and throws up her hands, as if she's throwing confetti into the air for an invisible parade.

"He's got a right," I say. "He's still alive. Besides, he *wants* to."

"He practically raised the kid, paying for all those schools when Daddy died. It makes sense he wants to go." Alice-James smiles. "Maybe Bo could even be best man, or give a toast."

"I think you're both crazy," Ma says. "How's Bo supposed to last a four hour car ride? He can't even sit up. By now, his cancer's got cancer."

The three of us lean in over a half-empty box of donuts, sipping our coffee from old stained mugs, pressing down so hard our elbows practically stick to the Formica tabletop. Our hands fidget with everything: packets of NutraSweet, unmatched spoons, a saltshaker, the plastic honey shape of a bear. It's seven a.m. and still so dark that you can't see past yourself in the window. So dark that you just have to trust the mountains are out there, springing up against a flat sky. Bo's dogs, Henny and Penny, are scratching their morning routine under unseen trees that have all gone brown with crisp November.

At this blind hour, every second is a leap.

Ma turns to me. "What're you supposed to do, load him up like a piece of luggage in the station wagon?"

"It's Andy," I say. "You know how much Andy means to him. Bo wants to say goodbye."

When I was nine, Alice-James woke me out of a deep sleep and told me to carry our baby brother from his bed down the stairs. He was half dreaming in my arms in the kitchen when she commanded me to push him out the door onto the driveway.

It was freezing cold. I was too afraid to say no.

Alice-James, thirteen at the time, ran around locking all the doors.

Andy finally woke up all the way, crying at the top of his lungs. He jiggled one doorknob after another, frantic.

I begged her to let him in. "I'll be your slave for a week."

"You?" Alice-James laughed, looking right through me. "You're nothing, Ginny Wojak. You can't even think for yourself."

By grade school, Andy would stare at himself in the mirror

for hours, trying to see what provoked Alice-James and me to call him names: stupid, ugly, sissy. Evenings, when our father came home, we locked ourselves in the bathroom, leaving Andy to fend for himself. He was the perfect target, cowering in corners or dropping to the floor, refusing to defend himself. Sometimes Daddy would just flop down on the floor too, drunk, carrying on about his own father. He'd pull Andy into his lap, kissing him with sloppy, parted lips—an apology.

The dogs scratch to be let in, and Alice-James turns to see who's there. I'm the one who gets up.

Outside, the first daylight glints through the mountains.

"You're letting in the cold," Ma says.

The dogs circle around, settling under the table to warm our ankles.

Each minute takes us that much closer to the hour Ma will go off to ladle turkey fricassee to hungry children at the elementary school and Alice-James will drive one town over to Procter & Gamble, where she heads up her own shift at the factory. She lives in the house where we grew up with Ma. Mornings, they drive the familiar roads from our old house to this one, the house where Bo and I live, where he grew up. After dinner, they drive the same roads back. It's our routine since Daddy died and Bo got sick. Here for dinner. The next morning, here for breakfast.

"Dead body in the back seat's got to be at least a felony." Ma puts out a match between her fingers.

"Give it a rest, Ma," says Alice-James. "It's not for you to say."

Ma shifts in her chair, looking tense in a long-sleeve shirt that says "Waynesboro Grammar School, Waynesboro, PA." She looks at me from the corner of her eye.

"I'd just as soon he didn't go," I say. "But how can I say no?"

She taps her Newport Lights on the table like she's answering my question in code.

Alice-James leans in. "You don't make the decisions, Ma. I think you know that by now."

In the quiet we can hear Bo's raspy breathing upstairs and the creaking of the bed whenever he shifts his weight.

"Daddy would object." Ma's final words whenever she's losing an argument, though Daddy's been dead for years.

Before he finally got sober, Daddy drove a school bus for nearly forty years, picking up the retarded kids from their programs and delivering them safely home. On the afternoons he escaped with a bottle of Beefeater into the back woods, Ma would send Alice-James on his three-o'clock route. Sometimes she sent me along with Andy in tow to keep an eye out. The older kids hated it when our father wasn't there, rolling and moaning like hedgehogs on the side of the road, some of them banging their helmets against the windows. They loved our father so much— his big welcoming grin, his easy girth that made you feel safe— we often had to hold some down so Alice-James could see out the rear view mirror.

Daddy started going to AA meetings after he was diagnosed with liver disease. Five weeks later he went into the hospital, fell into a coma, and refused to die. The doctors pressured Ma; the nurses gave her looks. No matter how hard Alice-James lobbied, though, Ma couldn't pull the plug. When his kidneys stopped working, he blew up like a water balloon, his skin nearly splitting at the creases.

Every morning she'd leave the house, determined, and every evening we'd arrive at the ICU and sit listening to the sound of Daddy's machines. His urine bag filled up with coffee grounds—"That's blood, Mrs. Wojak" the nurses told my mother. "Can't imagine he'd want you to let this happen to him."

After several weeks Daddy finally gave up and stopped breathing. He waited until four in the morning when everyone was home. The cause of death was listed as heart failure.

"Guess you wouldn't put *drunk* on the death certificate," said Alice-James.

After that Ma didn't want to be responsible for any more decisions. Her heart was broken, she said. She didn't care if we put him in his school bus and drove him into the river, long as we did it quickly.

Our first family vote was unanimous: cremation.

"Other families make decisions the normal way," Andy said the next Saturday, the three of us in the house cleaning out Daddy's things. (Back then we couldn't turn around without someone calling a referendum to make a decision: life insurance, charities, whether to sell the truck.)

"We're supposed to be swayed by your view of normal?" said Alice-James.

It had been delicate getting Ma out of the house, but Alice-James was determined. After a vote, Ma agreed to spend the day with Bo. He took her shopping in the afternoon, scrambled her eggs with hot sauce for an early supper in my kitchen and took her bowling with the League.

Armed with brooms and garbage bags, we worked in different parts of the house all morning, attacking from the basement on up, boxing everything we could, from clothes to tools to magazines. Alice-James could have found her way through blindfolded, but Andy roamed the hallways, lost, counting the days before he could leave us behind for college.

I was carrying a bag of old *National Geographic*s to the garbage cans under the back stoop when I found him brooding, chin resting on his knees.

"Don't listen to Alice-James," I said. "You're as normal as any of us."

"Do you remember our childhood?" Andy said. "Do you think about it?"

When he was in the fourth grade Andy announced at dinner that he wanted to marry the music teacher, Mr. Florentine. Daddy asked Ma to please pass the mashed potatoes. Ma pressed her lips together, advising Andy not to talk with his mouth full.

"Sometimes I remember," I said.

"Daddy hated me."

I said, "No more or less than he loved you, Andy. Or any of us."

"Hey, you two, come up here." We looked up to see Alice-James's fleshy face peering down from a window. "The empty bedroom," she said. Before I'd married Bo our senior year in high school and moved out, the empty room was where I slept.

We ran up the stairs. In my old room, relieved now of old high-school banners and photographs of Bo on the track team to make it comfortable for guests who never came, Alice-James stood muttering. "Daddy took his daily naps in this room. Help me move the bed."

We slid the single bed frame across the carpet and heard a clanking of glass by Alice-James's feet. Several dusty bottles skidded out from under the bedspread. Empties piled high as the hem on her long skirt knocked against her swollen ankles.

Andy eyed the labels: Listerine, Scope. "Mouthwash?"

"Last few months, he was drinking these," Alice-James said, holding up a bottle.

"Drinking?"

"Alcohol is alcohol."

"He wasn't drinking," Andy said. "The doctor said he couldn't."

She shrugged.

"Bo drove him to those meetings every week," I said. "Alcoholics Anonymous."

"Evidence is evidence," Alice-James said. She seemed relieved when we ran out of protests, giving us a minute to absorb the information. Daddy had always said she had the brains in the family.

"Okay, let's have a vote on this."

Andy was still five months shy of eighteen; according to Alice-James, who made the rules, his vote didn't count. Even so he voted with the majority to not tell Ma.

His first and only legal vote would be a few months later, for college: Penn State. Once he was gone, the voting became habit: forcing issues, building consensus, whittling wholly distinct opinions down to bottom lines. A single "yea" or "nay" on scraps of paper summed up our philosophies, folded in half and dropped in a shoebox, hoping for the best.

Andy moved on, but we remained, polling our way through life.

Me, Ma, and Alice-James gather around Bo's hospital bed in the front room upstairs after dinner.

"Time to call the question?" he asks. I can tell his head is aching by the way his eyes droop. I give him pills from one of the bottles lined up on the bureau.

Soon the medication kicks in. He smiles dopily and pats my hand.

Alice-James takes the only chair next to his bed.

"As we all know, Andy doesn't really want us to go to his

commitment thing…wedding, or whatever."

"A.J.!" Ma is perched on the foot of the bed. "No stacking the vote."

"I'm recapping, Ma. It's perfectly legal." Alice-James puts on her most innocent expression. "Although I do find it interesting that I'm the only one who can face facts around here: We embarrass Andy."

"I got an invitation says otherwise." Ma flashes a cream-colored card. Fancy letters say that Andy, our little brother, and Wilhelm Livingston, a complete stranger to us, invite us to a commitment ceremony celebrating their life together.

Alice-James snorts: "It doesn't mean they actually expect us to show up."

"You don't know that, Alice-James," I like to voice the opposition.

"Don't I?" Her voice is a sneer. "When's the last time Andy came for a visit? Or remembered a birthday? And since this brain thing with Bo, has he so much as sent a flower? Bo paid for every last thing that kid has since long before Daddy died, college, food, clothes, books—and what? Andy can't pick up the phone?"

"Okay, now," Bo says hoarsely. It calms us all.

Some people get sharp and angular when they are dying, mean like Daddy, but Bo has gotten even sweeter than usual. I see it when the union boys come hold their meetings, sitting on the floor around Bo's hospital bed, telling him plumber jokes, drinking beer, crying sometimes, big tough babies. Bo comes from a large family of plumbers. Like his father and his father's father, he is, and will be until he dies, a respected union steward in the Local 307.

"I thought guys like Andy were supposed to be sensitive," Alice-James says.

"I talked to him today, A.J." Ma peers across the room. "He wants us to stay over, spend the night."

"Is that right, Rusty?" Bo says. I slide onto the bed next to him, rubbing his arms.

Alice-James doesn't bat an eye.

"You remember that girl Andy brought home that one Christmas, Bo?" Ma keeps a steady gaze on Alice-James. "What was her name? We thought maybe he'd brought her home to marry."

"You thought," Alice-James says under her breath.

"The one with the hair?" I say.

"The lesbian?" Alice-James says.

Ma keeps talking: "Andy wants us to stay with her for the weekend. Ashley, I think it was. She has a house in New Jersey, somewhere nearby. But I told him not to go to any trouble; we were just coming for the day. And he said, 'What trouble is that, Mother?'"

"Thoughtful," Bo says affectionately.

"Something else, too," Ma continues. "He's changing his name."

"What's wrong with 'Andy'?" I ask.

"That's what I said!" Ma tilts her head. "And he goes, 'No, Mother, my last name.' He and this Wilhelm are hyphenating. That's what he called it. *Hyphenating.* Wojak-Livingston."

"You got to be kidding me." Alice-James barks out a cruel laugh.

Ma glances around the room to see how the news is going over.

"That's our boy!" Bo leans back on the pillow, smiling. "Got his own beat, his own drum, even his own drumsticks."

Ma laughs, too. Suddenly we all let go laughing, as if we have entered some lighter existence. Alice-James pulls a

Kleenex from her sleeve and holds it to her lashes as she rocks in her chair. Bo's laugh turns to coughing and we quiet down, watching him.

When his hacking doesn't stop, I push him into a sitting position and pound on his back until he can breathe again.

It takes two school board meetings and a petition three weeks before Andy's wedding for Alice-James to secure the school bus. *Superintendent was a friend of Daddy's from way back,* Alice-James reports for family minutes.

She draws maps with colored pencils to mark out the stops on the roads parallel to Route 6. The map includes the woods where Bo loved to go hunting with the dogs, the high school where Bo and I first fell in love, and a drive through the Endless Mountains on back roads, Bo's favorite place in the world.

The entire trip is off the beaten path, a kind of nature ride.

For every stop, Alice-James has put an asterisk. At the bottom of the page it says *Health Permitting.*

She tacks the map to the side of Bo's dresser. When we roll him on his side to check for bedsores, he reaches across the pillow, tracing the route with a fingernail. Ma stands in the doorway and shakes her head.

"You voted, too," I whisper, catching her by the arm.

"I voted for the wedding, not for carting Bo around."

"Same vote. You could have called for a friendly dispersal."

She sighs.

As she walks away I realize the family vote is a sham—another excuse to pretend someone else made you do it.

*

Jed, an orderly Alice-James used to date, gets the gurney for her as a favor, just like the hospital bed he salvaged from emergency room storage. He plans to rip out a few rows of seats to get it to fit in the bus.

"Another favor," Jed tells me the morning of the wedding, when he drags a friend over to help with the bus.

I pour them each a cup of coffee.

Alice-James pulls up in the old yellow school bus, swinging open the door machinery to let Ma out. The engine is loud enough to spook the dogs, who bark and whimper on the front step.

"Shut up, you two," Ma says from the bottom step of the bus. She looks like a small stooped child clinging to the rail, leaning her body out into the open air.

"Thank God your father's not alive to see this!" she says, coming into the kitchen.

I hand her two hanging bags for the actual ceremony: one with my dress and one with a suit for Bo. I've made a medical kit out of Bo's hunting bag: pills, water, nasal sprays, mucous pumps.

Alice-James is in sweatpants, a matching pink outfit with white racing stripes. "Ready?" she says. "How's Bo today?"

"Headache," I say, "but ready."

Jed takes the bags to the bus.

"All right," Alice-James says, "let's get this show on the road."

There's some trouble getting him down the staircase, but Bo wheels smoothly into the kitchen. "I miss this place," he says, making me wish I'd given the house a good cleaning.

Inside, without three quarters of its seats, the bus is cavernous. Alice-James and her hired hands wheel Bo in through the rear emergency doors. Rubber mats line the floor.

The metal is rusted, but there is plenty of room. We tie the gurney to a rig with rope.

Through the windows facing him, Bo can see the sky. He insists the dogs come along for company. "You can't bring those hounds to a wedding," Ma says.

Alice-James calls a vote. "They can stay in the bus. Who's in favor?"

It's unanimous with Ma's abstention. Even Jed and his friend raise their hands.

I whistle Henny and Penny onto the bus. They shimmy their red sleek bodies, huddling together in a small corner near Bo.

"Crazy damn bunch, you are," Jed says, standing in the driveway and waving us off by one o'clock sharp.

Alice-James leans out the window, restarting the engine.

Ma studies the five rows of vinyl benches, picks an aisle in front. I sit a little farther back, next to Bo.

Revving the engine, Alice-James pulls out of the driveway like a pro. "Just like the old days." She smiles at me in the rearview mirror.

I give her two thumbs up.

Bo reaches for my hand. I bend down to catch his words over the sound of the engine rumbling low through the rubber floor.

"The air smells so good," he says. It's been four months since he's been outside our bedroom. "And everything, everything looks great."

"Thank God your father's not here," Ma shouts over the loud engine.

"Amen to that," Alice-James calls.

"Alvin James Wojak, may he rest in peace." Ma waves her hand in front of her face.

It is a sunny day, but cold. We have worried all week about

the weather. In these parts, there's always a danger of snow.

"Think of this as a tribute to Daddy," A.J. says. "Or an apology for not pulling the plug while he was lying there all those months suffering."

Ma grabs the bottom edge of her seat as the bus rumbles. "I couldn't do it," she shouts over the engine. "I wanted to, but I couldn't."

"Well, I could have done it."

Bo says, "Not your fault, Rusty."

"I'd do it again exactly the same, too," Ma says. "Say what you will, but I'd rather live in that corner hospital room for months than let him go. I never loved anyone or anything as much as your father. Not even my children, though I'm sorry about that some days."

Alice-James sits high in the driver's seat, handling the gears with ease. She shifts her eyes in the rearview mirror, looking for Ma, who sinks low in her seat.

"Terrible love," Ma says.

At every checked and noted location on Alice-James's map, we vote to keep driving. Bo vomits once in a bucket Ma brought. "Told you so," Ma says under her breath. Still and all, he's in good spirits. For the two hours it takes riding parallel to Route 6, I administer pills, soothe Bo with a wet washcloth and wipe his brow. He's thirty-three—*Buddha Year*, Alice-James calls it. *The year Jesus died*, Ma says ominously. When I met Bo, he was fourteen; when I married him, he was eighteen. The doctors say he won't make it to thirty-four.

Alice-James leans her elbow out the window and hums to herself, scanning the back of the bus with eagle eyes. Ma curls up in her seat and snores for about an hour, rousing to complain about her bladder. A few minutes away from the Endless Mountains, the longest leg of our journey, Alice-James pulls up in front of a brick McDonald's for a pit stop and coffee to go with the lunch I've packed. It's a nice one with a pond out back.

Ma and Alice-James take coffee orders—three black with sugar; nothing for Bo—and head off to use the ladies room. I help Bo relieve himself into a plastic hospital bottle. There is very little urine, though it's been hours.

I peer out the window at the little pond. "We could feed the ducks."

Bo's eyes roll slowly up my face. "We could feed them Percocet."

Alice-James has left the motor running for warmth, but I can still see our breath mingling silver in the cold air between us. Bo's breath comes slow and labored.

"Maybe we should go back," I say.

"No such thing. Besides, it's good to have someone to say good-bye to. It's good to have somewhere to go. I was born in that house. Person shouldn't die in the same place they were born."

I let Henny and Penny run wild into the soft afternoon, scaring away all the birds. They bark at a family of ring-neck ducks and gallop, leading the way down the path near the water.

After I use the ladies room, we settle back in the bus, eating the sandwiches I made from leftover roast. "What did we get him?" Ma says, pointing at the elegantly wrapped flat rectangle leaning against the driver's seat.

"Yeah, what'd we get?" Bo hasn't eaten in several days.

"Remember my trip to Florence?" Alice-James sits in the middle of the vinyl seats, big and pink, rolling her hair in plastic curlers. "I met that man in Florence, a famous artist now."

"Oh, yes, José Whoosits!" Ma hugs her down jacket. "Put

the heater on, A.J."

"It was Pedro, Ma," Alice-James says, "And I'm not putting the heater on. We brought plenty of blankets for Bo. Why don't you use one?"

"You were so young, A.J., seventeen." Ma lights a cigarette.

Bo leans his head against me, hot with fever. I feed him pain medicine from a brown paper bag of pill bottles, and some water, which makes a gurgling noise against his lips.

"It's artwork," Alice-James says. "A charcoal drawing, a gift."

"A drawing?"

"It's a garlic on a black background."

Ma is skeptical. "How come I never saw it?"

"Sounds pretty," I say.

"I had it put in a big frame with lots of matting around it," Alice-James says.

Ma clears her throat. "What's with garlic?"

"It looks so real, papery-thin, you want to reach right out and touch it." She ignores Ma. "The card says, 'May your love be equally mysterious.'"

Bo looks up at me, smiling. "Sounds nice." I hold his thin face between my hands.

"I wanted to write, 'Love is like garlic; it really stinks.'"

Bo laughs.

"In California," she says, "they call garlic the stinking rose."

Ma sighs. "I don't get it."

"You don't have to," I say.

"Poetic," Bo closes his eyes.

Alice-James cups her hand over her ear. "What's that?"

"He says it's poetic," Ma shouts.

*

Three hours into the bus ride, Alice-James starts to fiddle with the heat, banging the top of the dashboard with her fist. By four-thirty, it starts to get dark, but we are nearly in New Jersey, where Andy and Wilhelm own a house.

The ceremony is being performed in their home promptly at six, we've been told, by a Methodist minister.

When I look out the window, all I see is the dim glow of day. Bo is lying still in the gurney, blankets piled high on top of him. He is resting his head on two pillows; his knees are bent in the middle. As he tries not to groan, Ma and Alice-James pretend not to hear him. The dogs rouse, coming over to nudge his thighs with their noses.

"Warm enough?" Alice-James shouts over the engine.

"Yes, ma'am."

Ma announces she needs a bathroom.

"Don't think so, Ma."

Ma sits up in her seat. Alice-James revs the coughing engine.

"A.J.!" Ma shouts over the engine, which is sputtering and sparking. The bus begins to kick. I hold onto Bo's head, to keep it from rocking off his pillow.

We're a half-hour from the New Jersey border on a small back road, when Alice-James pulls over to the shoulder. "Pee in the woods, Ma. We just ran out of luck with the engine."

Ma is standing in the aisle, next to the driver's seat, under a sign that says, Passengers are forbidden to ride in front of the white line. "What are we going to do now?"

Alice-James pulls the key from the ignition and turns in her seat. "Wait for help."

Forty minutes pass with no sign of a car. The evening starts to come in all ice and silver. Bo's lips are blue. "We'll freeze to death." Ma is shivering, pacing up and down the aisle.

"Relax, someone will come," Alice-James says.

"We need to get him somewhere warm," I say to Alice-James, when Bo's eyes are closed.

She nods. "Hey, let's play some rummy."

"I'm too cold," Ma says.

"A word game?"

"A.J., we're having an emergency." Ma stomps her sneaker against the back of her seat.

Bo coughs. We pile more blankets on him, and Alice-James and I take off our coats and place them on top.

Alice-James hefts herself out of the tight bus seat, touches the package, then tucks it under her arm, making her way slowly down the narrow aisle with Andy's present, a smooth, large rectangle wrapped in fancy gold paper with a yellow ribbon.

"You can't unwrap it," Ma says.

"Why not? I wrapped it. Come on," she says. "I'll put it back the way it was. It's really beautiful."

Henny and Penny's ears perk.

Kneeling next to Bo, Alice-James peels back the tape, lifts off the paper, revealing a background black as night with the slightest hint of a cross in the charcoal.

"Ma, get the bus light."

No one moves.

We are crowded around the head of Bo's gurney staring at the little drawing.

Ma whispers, "Oh, that's nice."

Alice-James stands up abruptly. "You can't hardly see it without the light on."

She is wrong. The garlic nearly glows; our eyes are swallowed up in veins and delicate buds: the ordinary, magnificent facts of existence. It's plain as anything, extraordinary.

"Like a rose," Ma says softly.

"A heart," I say.

Bo reaches out as if he might peel a piece of papery skin away, or put the bitter bud in his mouth. Alice-James fumbles around up front, producing light from a smashed plastic fixture on the ceiling. At nearly the same moment, headlights appear up the road, weak at first.

"I told you it wouldn't be long," Alice-James shouts.

Grabbing the frame from the seat, she tucks the gift back in its paper, stashing it behind the driver's chair. Yanking curlers from her hair, she pulls out each tendril. She runs her fingers through the tight blonde curls, pulling them down and shaking them out in a way that makes her look suddenly glamorous.

"Get out there, Ma, and start waving them down."

She winks at me, applying a few dabs of pink to her mouth. "A little lipstick never hurts." Producing a flare from the dashboard, she jumps down the steps, the entire bus rocking with her weight. A pink glow fills the bus as she sets the flare off in the street, then comes back in to look for her hairbrush.

Bo's eyes are closed.

"It's important," he says.

"We're going to get you someplace warm," I say.

"I'm warmer than I've ever been." He holds out his hand.

"We're getting you someplace warm, Bo," Alice-James says, poking her head through the bus doors before heading back outside. "Looks like Ma and me are going with this guy in his car up the road, and we'll come back with an ambulance."

Bo grabs my hand, and pulls at me weakly. "No, Ginny," he says.

Walking to the front, I motion Alice-James off the bus for a private conversation.

She steps back into the cold.

"Go to the wedding," I say. "Don't call an ambulance."

"Are you crazy? You'll freeze to death."

I hand Alice-James five twenty-dollar bills from my pocket. "You and Ma go."

Alice-James looks at the money, but doesn't take it.

"Tell Andy that Bo couldn't make it today."

Ma is standing in the dark behind Alice-James. "That's the first true thing anyone has spoken all day."

"Tell him good luck. Bo wished he could say so himself."

The car waiting on the shoulder of the road honks its horn.

Alice-James stares at me, deflated, her mouth slightly ajar. "We voted."

"It's my life, Alice-James." I walk to the back of the bus, the dogs on my heels, and throw open the emergency doors, pulling the luggage out. Ma stands with her arms open, ready to catch her dress. The dogs bark at her. Ma gets into the car. As the stranger revs the engine, she sticks her head out the passenger seat window. "Let's go," she shouts to Alice-James who is still standing in the doorway up front.

"Don't forget the garlic." I hand Andy's gift to Alice-James. She looks at me, puzzled, frowning.

I tell her, "I'm not nothing, you know."

Finally, the car pulls away. A weak stream of light from the broken plastic fixture and the dying pink glow of Alice-James's flare are all we have. I sit listening to the panting of the dogs and the sounds of evening, which seem silent in the absence of everyone else.

"Your life went somewhere," I say, staring out the window.

I look away from Bo and his absolute stillness, picturing Ma and Alice-James in their best clothes. Andy will take Ma in his arms and give her a secret hug in the foyer, telling her she's the most beautiful girl at the wedding. Alice-James will report back in full detail, her feelings hurt by a dozen different comments, including mine. I think of how it will be when it's just the three of us—me, Ma, and Alice-James—dividing and redividing our loyalty, making grids out of our lifelines. Three is not enough to make a vote, and some things are beyond our jurisdiction.

I hold my own hand, waiting in the dark for the snow to come at last.

A LINE
OF
E.L. DOCTOROW

A LINE OF E.L. DOCTOROW

WHEN DREAMS COME TRUE, disappointment always follows. *Restriction of the heart,* Lorena thinks, sensing that she is the perfect example.

Of course, there was never any question about the house; she'd wanted it. And the husband with a ready-made family; recently, even, a baby of her own. And yet on certain days she cannot seem to breathe.

Twice a week, she manages to distract herself at a gourmet shop, selling overpriced champagne grapes and figs the color of lipstick to people like herself, wealthy.

She's gotten used to thinking this way.

The job is really just research for starting her own market: *Lorena's Fruit.* She has a degree from Smith, for goodness sake, and credits toward her MBA from Yale. Besides, she's always wanted her own business, though several years ago, when she couldn't find a decent distributor for her greeting card venture (pine needles on homemade paper), her interest began to wane.

"Find an au pair," the other Connecticut mothers say. "There's more tennis that way."

Lorena does find an au pair, a perfectly suitable one from a decent family in the city, but she does so simply for the challenge, a labored search through haystacks and something to talk about to friends.

Early on a Friday morning, not even ten, she is late picking the girl up at the train station. She's mad at herself for being disorganized, for being overly eager to see the young woman, whose love affair created a scandal with an assistant professor at Lorena's own alma mater, perhaps a delightful distraction after all.

Lorena sees the girl on the train platform, where she is standing innocently, overnight bag tucked casually under her arm, as if she'd never even heard of love-gone-wrong. Taking a sharp left into the parking lot, Lorena halts the minivan and lays on the horn.

"Allison?" she says through the open window. The girl is surprisingly young, round-faced and freckled, a swatch of red hair, a turned-up nose. "Sorry we're late. Joshy slammed his finger in the door."

"Oh dear," Allison says. "I hope he's okay."

"Indestructible." From her own rearview mirror, Lorena sizes up the Spencer children as if with a stranger's eye; they seem vague to her this way, their heads small and gourd-like, easy to harm. "They all are."

Allison takes a quick glance back at the children, then opens the door.

"Get in," Lorena says, cheerfully. "Say hello, boys."

Eric, her husband Babe's oldest son, is nearing puberty. Soon there'll be girls to contend with, hormones, and angst. Teetering on the edge of acne, Eric waves a hopeful hand at the new babysitter, lifting out of his seat to get a better look. On his left is Josh, Babe's youngest son, a boy who reeks of sweat and insecurity, who taps his hands involuntarily against hard surfaces. He slouches in the prized seat by the window, won by virtue of asthma, and twitches through the introduction. In the far seat is Little Jake, drooling peacefully, strapped in, head lolling, half-asleep.

Lorena tries to imagine how Allison might see them. *Amoebic?* None of Babe's children have made it unscathed through their respective mileposts of danger: infancy, boyhood, pre-adolescence. Their thin bodies appear innocent and unassuming.

They spend their days at the mercy of other people: teachers, tutors, babysitters. She watches Josh, another woman's child, as he continuously raps his knuckles on the window, as if to contain himself, to find some rhythm of calm.

The human cranium, Lorena knows, is not fully formed until age seven. She wonders briefly if that other mother, the inattentive one, or some previous sitter—au pair—is responsible for the boy's twitch and obsession with computers. Dropped him on his head? Pressed a thumb into his soft spot?

At least it wasn't her.

Allison fumbles with the seat belt, and Lorena reaches over to help. Her hands flutter like white moths at the girl's hip, then up to her own mouth, wistfully, as if searching for a source of light.

This visit had been Lorena's idea. *Why not come and see how you like us?* And now Lorena is nervous.

Allison smiles with the ease of unflappable youth.

Immediately, Eric starts his inquisition: "Guess how many brothers I have?"

Allison smiles. "Two."

"Wrong!" Eric crosses his arms over his painfully skinny chest, smirking at Lorena in the rearview. "The answer is one of each! I have a half brother, a whole brother, and a step brother."

Lorena rolls her eyes emphatically. "His father taught him that."

"Oh," Allison says. Lorena sees her look doubtfully at the

three children in the back seat, searching for resemblance.

She ploughs headlong through the unasked question. "Eric and Joshy have been with me for quite some time, three years now. Their real mom lives in Tampa. I always tell Babe, if he ever wants a divorce, he'll have to leave the boys with me. Isn't that what I tell your father, boys?"

"Yup," Eric says.

Lorena flicks on the blinker in the middle of a turn.

"Okay," Allison says, poised and smiling, turning toward Eric. "If Josh is your whole brother, and Baby Jake is your half brother, then who is your step brother?"

"Aaron," Eric answers eagerly. "He doesn't live with us anymore. We sent him away to boarding school, right Lorena?"

Lorena laughs. "Aaron is my first born from my first marriage. He has a good heart, really. A little impulsive is all." For a moment, she considers telling the truth about all the diagnoses from school experts: ADD, AHD, mild Autism, personality adjustment disorder. "I guess you could say he's had some difficulties along the way, mostly competitive feelings toward Eric and Josh, even Babe. And it was really tough on him when I got pregnant with Baby Jake. It's hard to blame him, though. He was used to having me all to himself, then all of sudden it was like the Brady Bunch, only not so happy, you know? He lives with his Dad for now out on Block Island."

Eric leans into the front seat. "My Dad didn't like Aaron's attitude."

She eyes her stepson in the rearview mirror. "Your father can be a little impetuous, himself, Eric." She laughs again, self-conscious now. "Anyway, our decision to board Aaron at Andover has more to do with his future than anything else."

"Does Mr. Spencer always take such long business trips?" Allison asks.

Babe is scheduled to stay in Germany through the summer, a brief respite for Lorena, which must feel like an eternity to someone as young as Allison. She seems lost in her dreamy observation of Connecticut through the window, Lorena notices.

"I mean," Allison says, rephrasing, "how do you do it?"

"Babe's pretty driven," Lorena says, "which means he'll pick up and go halfway around the world if it helps Spencer Enterprises."

"The Starship Enterprise," Eric mumbles from the back seat. He crashes several shiny objects, toys, together in front of him, making battle noises.

"I don't really know how I do it." Lorena smiles at the windshield. She notices the strange afternoon light, as if a hook of sunlight has pierced through her eyelid, obstructing normal vision. Everything is a blur in the syrupy days of early summer; even the Connecticut pines appear pliable and huddled. "I hire you, I guess."

The rest of the drive home, Lorena tries to envision Connecticut through fresh eyes. Houses whiz by, surprisingly unattractive, opulent even. When she herself first arrived in Greenwich, there were overwhelming manicured lawns to contend with. "The Emerald City," she had remarked. The area is woodsy and dim—nothing like what Lorena was used to when she quit her job as a copywriter, married Babe, and moved from Manhattan. That he chose her of all the people in the office still seems amazing to Lorena and sometimes, when she is honest, terrible.

The pine trees—she noticed this right away, nearly first thing—look like poles, about as natural as lampposts, tall and spindly with an awkward triangle of green above the roofs. She'd mentioned it to Babe, asking if Connecticut grew them that way on architectural principle. Back then, the entire new world seemed affected, though now she barely notices.

"I loved Smith," Lorena says to fill up the silence. "Of course, I graduated in the 80s, which is a long time ago now. What year are you?"

"Class of 1998," Allison says.

Lorena rests her elbow out the window, enjoying the warm breeze and conversation. She wonders how Allison must see her: Big boned and medium framed? She thinks of herself as moving through the world with an illusion of elegance, a concept that may not translate easily. A Norwegian face distracts from her flaws: square jaw, big gums, short neck. Lorena wonders if her defects are apparent to Allison, whose attention she is having trouble keeping.

"I was a mathematics major," Lorena offers; "That's how I know your friend's mother who recommended you. Mary Gardener Hilton. Her little sister was my roommate. She could talk me into anything. I literally majored in Math because Lizzy Gardener was an Algebra whiz. Can you believe that?"

Allison laughs.

Why am I talking so much? Lorena wonders, but what she says is: *"Tempis fugit."*

"Don't tell me, Lizzy Gardener was good at Latin, too?"

"Absolutely." Lorena laughs. "The things we did for love."

An awkward silence unnerves Lorena—perhaps she's gone too far—perhaps in the 90s women at Smith no longer routinely fall in love with their roommates.

Eric capitalizes on the pause in conversation by leaning into the front seat, between the driver and her passenger.

"Dad turned breakfast into a meal of champions," he says. "And he made Slinky a national pastime. He was a junior copy writer for the Egg McMuffin, which was before burgers did breakfast."

"Walking billboard," says Lorena to Allison. "You know, you're shorter than I expected."

Allison blushes.

Lorena draws her shoulders up, concentrates on turning down the gravel road to the Spencer house, and better yet on keeping her mouth shut. *Try not to frighten little lambs,* she thinks. As they head deep into the familiar shaded lane, Lorena marvels at how quickly she has adjusted to Allison's presence, a new member of an old family with a tradition of adding and subtracting participants. She is happy to have the girl snap into the space left by Babe, happy to have an added appendage. A new distraction to appreciate.

They pull in the driveway of Babe's classic farm colonial. Lorena throws the car into park.

"Okay, boys," Lorena says, "let's try to make this one last for a change."

Eric bubbles, "Yeah! We buried the last babysitter in the back yard!"

Lorena takes a deep breath, looking briefly in the mirror. Blue-green eyes gleam back at her; a French braid holds her hair out of her face to reveal just how natural and Connecticut the whole entire world can be. She pulls the key from its ignition.

"Home sweet home," she says, practically shouting.

At the end of a weekend that includes the pool, a trip to the library, an impromptu stop at the video arcade, food shopping, two trips to the mall, and lunch at a fancy restaurant, Lorena and Allison sit in the kitchen. Sunday evening. Lorena has convinced her to take a morning train home, has been solicitous, flattering even. They slide a movie in the VCR for Eric and Josh and settle Jake in his highchair with a plate of peas and fish sticks. Allison pours them a glass of wine at Lorena's urging.

"Cheers," Lorena says, "you made it through your first two days."

Lorena wonders if she's being too pushy, but she has enjoyed the girl's company. She feels alive again, as if somehow she's forgotten all about friendship with women—not counting the stiff creatures Connecticut grows to mother and marry. Lorena wants real live chatter and lunches, companionship.

After baths and bed, which Allison manages without fight, flood, or tantrum, they sit on the back porch in the dark, stretching their legs over the wicker furniture. The lawn to the back woods is a messy tangle of toys and bikes only visible by the glints of the large New England moon. Inside, the house is also a mess. Florence, the housekeeper, comes again in the morning. Still, surprisingly, Lorena can tell that Allison is comfortable. She feels fine, she tells herself. She'll work out fine. She has put in a good effort, handled the problems as well as possible with Lorena's help and without it.

"So what do you think of them?" Lorena sits in patio furniture she's picked out herself. It is white wicker with a pillow of soft mauve.

"You've got a great crew."

"They're pretty good kids," Lorena says. "Though Joshy has real problems."

Allison nods.

Lorena is always slightly shocked when anyone acknowledges her stepson's issues. She often feels like reminding everyone in the room that he's not her kid. "I don't know what to do about it. I try to reassure him. He misses his mom, you know. He was attached to her. It's terrible. The woman doesn't even call on his birthday. He seems interested in you, though.

That was a surprise. How was he, today?"

"Okay, I think, though there was an incident at the pool." Allison pauses to crunch absently on a carrot. "Screaming at the top of his lungs."

Lorena feels a sweet terror rising in her throat, then realizes it is just the effect of the wine warming her through. She pours a second glass. "What happened?"

"He said one of the other kids tried to drown him. Garrison something."

"Garrison Foley," Lorena swings back in her lawn chair, "a real little bastard. Well, no wonder. He probably did. The kids around here are privileged little brats, but they're rough. I've seen them reduce grown-ups to tears. Just like their fathers. They're the products of an unbelievable life."

They are silent for a minute, listening to the sound of the crickets. Lorena thinks she has been too forceful about the neighbors' children. She tries to think of a thing softer to say, some way to take it back.

"It was strange though," Allison says. "No one saw anything. All the kids were on the other side of the pool, and even Garrison Foley was standing on the diving board."

"That's not good." Lorena hears her own voice far away in the night.

"It's like he has hurt feelings," Allison says. "And doesn't know how else to express them. So, he makes up these little scenes."

"You think he makes things up?" Lorena sips her wine casually.

But Allison merely repeats herself. "Yeah, but as an expression of pain. Not exactly real, but not exactly not-real, either."

Lorena stretches in the dark, listening to the reassuring

chirp of crickets. *Maybe he does make it all up,* she thinks. "I need to take him to a neurologist about that obsessive finger-tapping. It wasn't so bad when he only did it on top of his own desk. Now, he reaches right out and touches people like that. I swear he's going to come home with a black eye one day."

In the dark, Lorena admires Allison's red hair, her decisiveness and obvious intelligence.

"I think it's going to be a good summer, after all," she says.

When Lorena first accepted that Babe had chosen her, she moved into the Midtown Sheraton Hotel without telling her roommate, or her husband, who was in the middle of divorcing her. Babe lived in Lyme, Connecticut with his wife at the time. The wife was a woman somehow named Bridey, who was ill in ways Babe never could actually explain. He was lonely and wanted Lorena whenever he could get her, whenever he could escape and spend an hour, an evening, the night. He wanted her all the time, he said. And she didn't mind the luxury that came with it. Maids to make her bed, dry cleaning service at the door, all meals delivered. She liked that no one lived in a hotel, not even her, though for a solid year, it's where she spent her time. Every so often, she returned to her own apartment near Prospect Park; her husband had just finished medical school and moved to the country. He'd taken Aaron with him, except for the summers when she got him.

"A lot of traveling," she'd say to Sylvia, her roommate, a strange woman with a lisp. For some reason, Lorena felt compelled to haul an empty suitcase home, shower and catch up on sleep, then haul it back into a cab heading uptown.

"Market research," she told the woman, who wouldn't probably have cared either way.

Babe teased her mercilessly about the pretense. "What do you care what other people think?" he wanted to know. But she didn't like being the other woman.

And now here she is again.

Perhaps she ought to have expected it, coming home early from tennis and finding him there like that with Allison. She ought to have anticipated the pattern, the familiar circadian rhythm of Babe Spencer and his predictable conquests. Now, Lorena chastises herself for being surprised. What has happened could be written in a tawdry novel: Babe returning home from abroad in August, unexpectedly early, dampening everyone's spirits, though not Allison's, Lorena notices. The observation stings her to numbness with rejection, though she knows she's acting foolish, like a young lover who hasn't yet known passion. Still she recognizes that something has been taken away. To keep her mind off it, she keeps herself busy with Josh's doctor's appointments, psychiatrists, and trips to the pharmacy for Ritalin. She books tennis games in the middle of the day.

"I see you're really taking advantage of the new girl," her friends say.

Is she?

She can't help the constant feeling that she should be home with her fingers on the pulse of the life being lived there. She makes elaborate family dinners, enlisting Allison's help, trying to keep her attention. Babe sinks into bad moods, snarls at the children, grumbles around the house. In the morning, he refuses to let Joshy take the sheet off the birdcage until he has gone to work.

"Can't stand that racket," he says.

Joshy acts as if he doesn't care. "It's still dark out, in bird world."

Lorena can't blame Babe, exactly. He's lost two major deals

in Germany, and there are snags in a third. These are harsh blows coming on the heels of his latest venture, a novel start-up company to sell medicine directly to patients. The FDA closed the operation down, a year after incorporation. Lorena has gotten used to hearing him begin all phone conversations with the same old line, "Let me tell you a story, Bob." The saga is about a little guy with a big idea, who is so down and out, trying to get his business up and running that he goes to Las Vegas to gamble payroll and wins big. "Ever heard of a little place called IBM," Babe says, reeling in the fish. It's hard to know anymore if the story is even true. Babe lies to win, a principle applicable in all situations.

To make life easier, Lorena simply steers clear, avoiding all but the most circumspect contact, except for the night of his return. They made love on the sofa, during which she found herself silently disappointed. She had to look away from his soft white mounds of flesh rising symmetrically to nipples, forced herself to concentrate on the wiry silver hair of his beard mixed with black in order to come. She's not sure how things have evolved to this point, but she knows making love with Babe in their home in Connecticut is nothing like making love in a hotel. She toys with the idea of taking him away for a weekend. Maybe even booking a suite at the Sheraton, but she seems to have no energy. Isn't interested, in fact. She spends a lot of time reading about parakeets and talking to Josh, who finally picks the perfectly colored bird, blue-green azure, which they buy in the pet store. She thinks it might help him to have something to care for.

She likes how the children have taken to Allison. Eric, in particular. Even Josh sometimes responds to her. He let her name the new parakeet: Cloud. Now that school has started, they seem to rely on her even more, and Lorena likes how she is with the baby.

In the back yard, after a tennis cancellation, Lorena watches Allison help Eric take black and white photographs with his new camera.

From behind a tree, Babe appears as if from nowhere. *He's not at work,* Lorena thinks, trying to remember the last time she's seen him in broad daylight. He's helping Eric. But something about the equation doesn't match up, and she feels compelled to follow quietly into the yard, leaving Josh alone, where she can see him through the window watching TV in the living room with the baby playing quietly in his pen.

She slips out the back porch and down the path toward the creek, glancing nervously toward the house, as if watching the back door will keep something bad from happening. No one catches sight of her out of the corner of an eye as she approaches, moving from one birch tree to the next, remaining hidden. They are helping Eric set up leaves and some stones for a still life. The air is chilly for October.

"It looks dumb," Eric complains. There's a pile of jackets—Allison's, Joshy's, Eric's—on the woodsy ground to her left.

"Your father will fix it." Allison looks up in Babe's direction, pointing with her chin.

"Daddy, please!" Eric wheels around. "Will you? Will you help me?"

Babe steps out from behind the tree: "Keep your voice down."

It is strange to see Babe behind the house, his sleeves rolled up, his suit jacket—where? Lorena looks around, spots it hanging from a tree branch; all day Lorena has been aware of a faint buzzing behind her skin. All day, she's felt a certain presence like something electrical, pressing into her stomach.

Babe fusses with the camera.

"Go back and get the pod for this in my office."

Eric takes off like a colt. "Be right back. Don't start without me!"

Babe fidgets with the camera, focusing in on Allison. "Want to pose?" he says. He pulls the camera away from his face. "Do you know who Emma Goldman is?"

Allison looks at him. (Lorena takes a deep breath.) "Of course I do."

"Well, at the end of her life, Emma Goldman, a confirmed revolutionary, conceded that reform had a place in the world. Do you know why?"

Allison shakes her head.

Lorena knows; it's a story she's heard a million times, a story he uses when he's closing a deal.

"She was visiting America one last time toward the end of her life, and she went to a factory, here, where she observed the incredibly abhorrent conditions of children working. This was before child-labor laws of course."

"And?"

And you son of a bitch, Lorena thinks.

"And it was extremely wise of her to change her mind like that, to realize that there are merits to improving a bad situation. Even an impossible situation. In her case, it was capitalism, for which the only true solution would be a social revolution. Still, she realized once and for all that improvement matters. Quality of life. You mustn't be rigid."

"Bread and roses," Allison says.

"Very good," Babe Spencer smiles.

"My great-aunt led that strike," Allison says. (*I'm sure she did*, Lorena thinks.)

"But what does this have to do with anything?"

"Given the impossible situation," Babe Spencer says, "I'd

say it has to do with everything."

He stares at her—long, hard, piercing. Lorena shifts her position, crouches down now, puts her head in her hand and tries to think.

"Allison?" Babe says.

"What?"

Lorena looks up.

"Unbutton your blouse." He is focusing the camera on her.

"Wait," he says. "First, undo your braid."

She moves her hands through her hair, then to the metal buttons of her chambray shirt, unbuttoning slowly.

Don't do it, Lorena thinks. Over her shoulder, she can see the house, but none of her boys.

She wonders if Allison is thinking the same thing.

"He'll be back," Allison says.

"Pull up that T-shirt," he says. "I want to look at you."

When she lifts her shirt to the brisk air, he snaps three quick biting photos, without saying a word.

"Beauty matters," he says.

It does, Lorena thinks, captivated as much by the dreadful situation as she is by Allison, who stands mannequin-like, lifting her shirt and showing off her porcelain skin, her delicate nipples puckered in the cold.

She can hear the sound of her own breath speeding up.

Letting the camera hang around his neck, Babe moves in for the kill. He jams his torso against her, pulling her in, slipping his hand quickly into the place where her jeans gap away from her flat stomach. He sucks on her lips, and she responds.

Oh, Allison, Lorena thinks, knowing he has slipped his finger inside her, where by now for certain she is wet and warm.

"Did you know this was going to happen?" he says, barely pulling away. "Did you know from the moment you saw me?

The moment you knew my favorite author was your favorite author. Doctorow. And Marxism? Did you think you could ignore such a connection? I knew. I could see it in your eyes the first time. It was inevitable. You knew it, didn't you?"

Say no, Lorena thinks, as she watches.

But Allison cannot answer.

"Doctorow said that we need writers as witnesses to this terrifying century. Are you terrified, Allison? Because I am."

Allison pulls away and quickly tucks in her shirt, searching for something to say. "I never heard that quote before."

It is just like Babe to research these things, or more accurately to have his secretary find these things out. Everyone saw Allison reading the Doctorow book; her school textbook on Marxism has been on the kitchen table all month. It's how Babe manages to seduce the world with his world-class advertising campaigns. Lorena wants to scream and warn the girl. She is breathing so hard in the cold that she has a headache.

Babe pulls out the film with the photos he's just snapped and tosses it in the air for Allison to catch. She puts it in her pocket, looking over her shoulder. Lorena watches Josh, not Eric, loping unevenly through the leaves. She wants to stand up and throw herself at his mercy, to tackle him to the ground, and cover his eyes. She wants to save him from everything, to make him stop twitching.

"What's the matter?" Allison asks shouting across a very short distance to Josh. Lorena recognizes the sound of panic rising in her throat.

He stands there without his jacket, trembling.

"Well, Josh?" Babe said, coolly, "What is it?"

Eric shows up, behind him, carrying the baby over one arm and the tripod for his camera over the other.

"Hey," he says to Josh, "Why'd you leave Baby Jake alone in

there? He was bawling."

The baby is wet-eyed, shivery in the cold; Eric hands him over to Allison.

Lorena makes her escape, down toward the creek and circling back up on the other side of the house, so she can slide by the van, as if she's just arrived home.

She stands in the garage listening for a moment.

"Did you remember your medicine today?" she hears Babe saying as he stomps his feet at the back porch, cuffing Josh lightly on the ear. "You got to remember it, son. It'll help you focus."

Josh doesn't answer.

"Lets get you inside before we freeze." Allison wraps the baby in her coat, and reaches out for Josh's hand.

"Now I'm sick," Josh whines. "You made me sick."

All evening Josh complains to Lorena about his fever, saying it is Allison's fault. Allison responds, apologizing profusely, until Lorena shows her the thermometer fresh from Josh's mouth. 98.6.

Lorena should fire the girl, though she did nearly the exact same thing to Babe's third wife, though not in the woman's house, the woman's bed. She wondered if given the opportunity, she would have.

At dinner, Babe's teasing grows tense. A sign Lorena recognizes that he perhaps believes himself to be in love and cannot bear the humiliation of the weakened state. He stretches, reaching for the salt.

"You have dandruff?" he asks Allison, "Don't you use a conditioner?"

He keeps his blue eyes steadily on target. Lorena notices

Allison flinch. Perhaps she can save her from this sort of thing. She sympathizes. It's not so bad to be someone's secret protector.

"Babe!" she reaches across and slaps his arm. "She does not have dandruff! Why would you say such a thing?"

A minute passes before Babe releases the girl from his barbed-wire gaze. Lorena snaps a cloth napkin from her lap into the air.

Lorena remembers what it's like to be caught off guard, when, accustomed to Babe's secret tenderness, one is ambushed by his public rage. In Lorena's case the affection was bestowed in the restroom at business luncheons, at her office after dark, and once in the hallway before the morning staff arrived. She wonders where it was offered to Allison. Maybe in the attic or in his office upstairs on the Berber rug, out back in the woods, after sending the boys on ahead to the little stream behind the house. Maybe Babe sneaks home in the middle of the day, pressing her up against the bookshelf in the baby's room, while the boys are down the hall. Maybe her own little Jake sleeps through the urgency of their sweaty motions.

"What's the matter with you?" Babe asks Josh. Lorena turns to see Josh's mouth falling open, mute. Everyone tenses, even Eric, as if sniffing the air for danger. Josh's hands move slowly like flies in winter. "A bus could come crashing through the kitchen, and you'd miss it!" Babe says. "Straighten up."

Eric stares at Allison's shoulder, but she's brushed it clear of the invisible white flakes, Lorena notices. Excusing herself from the table, she stands in the enormous, glinting stainless steel kitchen, looking around carefully, as if trying to regain her bearings.

*

After dinner, Allison goes to her room. A little reading to stay caught up on for school, she says, perhaps eager for her return spring semester.

The baby starts to cry. "I've got him," Lorena says. "You go." She rocks her son, her baby boy, in little half circles, and smiles.

Overhead, she can hear Allison putting the boys to sleep, and Babe in his office. When the baby is asleep, she puts him in his crib and tiptoes down the long hall back to Allison's room. *The maid's quarters*, Lorena reminds herself.

Lorena peeks her head in the room, not sure of what she's going to say. "You can't take Babe seriously."

Allison nods, staring at an open textbook on her desk. Lorena sits on the corner of the bed, within arm's length of Allison. Lorena sighs, picking up a brush and running it through Allison's auburn hair.

"Such a beautiful color," she murmurs.

"Dandruff," Allison says.

"Of course not." Lorena puts her arms around Allison. "Please don't leave us. You're the best thing that's happened to me in a long time."

"You know, one time I brought this woman home from school for Sunday dinner," Allison says in a slightly confessional tone, "and she helped get my nephew into Princeton, which is where she went to undergrad. And my brother said to her, *I was wondering why you were here all the time.*"

Lorena squints trying to follow the thread. "That sounds rude. Why was she there all the time? A friend, or more than that?"

"Well, that's the thing. He didn't want to know. He never asked the real question. And no one gets invited to the family dinner, unless they're really family."

"Well was she? Was she your family?"

Allison leans back slightly, almost imperceptibly, into Lorena's beating heart. *I forgive you,* Lorena thinks, remembering how the meanness of others can be a mystery when you're young. The heat of Allison's body reminds Lorena of something. Allison turns slightly in Lorena's arms, parts her lips to speak; their faces are alarmingly close. "She was important to me," Allison says.

They look at each other for another long moment, neither one speaking, until there's a knock at the door.

Lorena gets up quickly, smoothing her slacks.

"Come in," Allison says. The door swings open. Babe is standing in the hallway, smiling.

Lorena pushes past him. "I hope you've come to apologize."

Babe steps aside as she leaves the room.

"Goodnight, darling," he says quietly.

After Lorena lost custody of Aaron, she'd had a cancer scare that turned out to be harmless cysts, one of which had burst, causing unspeakable pain. She made an appointment with the gynecologist, who scheduled a sonogram. The day of her appointment, she'd had the usual case of nerves anticipating the grisly affair of spreading her legs for cold instruments. She could hear the nurses talking. *What was the young woman's last name again? Oh, wait, here it is. No, that's not it.* Ordering lunch: sushi and shrimp tempura. The more the invisible nurses behind the wall talked, the more nervous Lorena became.

They're never going to see me sitting out here, she thought, panicking, *they're never going to remember.* A quieter, more insidious thought came: *I have cancer. I'm going to die.*

Lorena burst into tears with *People* magazine lying open in her lap.

A pregnant woman to her right said, "Oh dear, are you all right?"

Another older woman, who probably did have cancer, went up to the Plexiglas window and knocked with her wedding ring. "Hey! Hey!" she said. "Can someone actually wait on us?"

Out the nurses came, a gaggle of white geese, swarming to bring Lorena back to a small, windowless examining room. Hesitant to take off her clothes, she cried even harder, silently, her mouth open, lungs straining.

"Are you all right? Are you okay, dear? Why don't you drink some water."

The sudden intense tending after their indifference made Lorena want to run away, the cancer surely eating a path through her ovaries. Instead, she stripped off her clothes and got into the stirrups.

After leaving Babe and Allison alone in the maid's quarters, Lorena checks on the boys—all of them sleeping—and remembers that particular kind of silent crying.

"Will you stay for Thanksgiving?" Lorena asks. She's feeling desperate. "You've become a member of the family."

They are in the kitchen, bright track lighting fighting off the impending winter dark. Yellow beams bounce off the large stainless sink, gourmet tools hanging from the walls and ceiling. Lorena feels comforted by Allison's presence, and by knowing the whereabouts of everyone in her household. Allison is freshly showered, which makes Lorena relax with the knowledge that the stain of her husband's touch has been washed away with expensive soaps.

This is her favorite time of day, alone together. And yet, somehow Lorena wants more than just the facts. She knows the bare minimum: that Allison grew up in a three-bedroom apartment near the projects on 106th Street. Her father is a spiritual and political leader, whom the *New York Times* called "radical" and "charming" for his loyalty to local communities. Babysitting in Connecticut isn't exactly an expected stop on Allison's journey, though her father approves of a semester off campus working with people, whether rich or poor. Her older sister teaches starving children in rural Central America. Her brother is Thomas Bentley, the only white city official ever to be elected to a primarily non-white district, still quaintly referred to as Spanish Harlem. And something lurid happened to Allison at Smith, involving a female professor and a public scandal.

Lorena places tiny cooked potatoes around an already-roasted chicken that she bought in town, while Allison assembles a salad. "I'll probably go to Manhattan. My family has a kind of traditional get together. Unless, of course, you need me?"

"Oh, please have dinner with us." Lorena takes down a stack of plates. "The boys love you so much. I don't know what I'd do without you."

Babe is faxing abroad or sulking over spreadsheets in his office upstairs. Lorena takes the opportunity to lavish attention on Allison, plying her with a few sips of white wine.

"Maybe," Allison says. "I'll have to do some fancy footwork with my mother."

"Let me talk to her." Lorena's eyes are bright. She puts her hands on Allison's waist, smiling down at her. "You absolutely must spend the holiday here with us. I simply won't take no for an answer."

Allison nods, twisting slightly out of Lorena's loose embrace. From the corner of her eye, she can see Babe standing in the shadow by the back stairway, watching.

That night, much to Lorena's surprise, Babe rolls over to

Lorena. "Do you want her?" he whispers. "Show me how you want her."

Silently then, passionately, they make love for the first time in months.

Lorena's son Aaron arrives early for Thanksgiving. His father drops him off the night before, driving off in the dark without so much as a honk of the horn. *Bastard*, Lorena thinks. He ought to at least have come in and said hello. Lorena is alarmed at her son's appearance; he has gained twenty pounds and a severe acne problem.

"We can go to a dermatologist while you're here," she says. It's probably not the first thing you should say to a child who was taken away from you, to a child who lives with his father. "You look strapping."

"I'm not going to any doctor," Aaron says. When she tries to give him a hug, he escapes from her arms, which is probably for the better. She notices a kind of illness odor; perhaps he hasn't bathed in weeks.

Babe does not come down for dinner.

The next morning Aaron is in the kitchen before Lorena, who nearly stumbles over him with the baby in her arms. Aaron doesn't speak to his mother; he grunts at Allison, who makes the coffee. This is his greeting. Lorena hugs him and ruffles his hair, hoping for a whiff of soap.

"Tell me every little thing that's going on, Aaron." She pours milk in his cereal, and sits close.

"I'm flunking out," he says. "I got kicked off the soccer team, and I punched my math teacher in the face."

This is his father's fault, Lorena thinks.

"Oh, be serious, will you?" She tries to smile deeply into his eyes. "You got four C's and a B-. Hardly flunking; I got my copy of your interim report card last week."

"Don't believe everything you read," Aaron says.

Lorena grimaces. "Did you see how big your baby brother is getting?"

Baby Jake is smashing Cheerios into the tray on his highchair.

"Huge," Aaron says without looking up.

"And what do you think of our girl, here?" Lorena catches Allison's wrist when she breezes by to bring her a hot mug of coffee.

Aaron opens his mouth, showing the half-chewed corn flakes.

"Yes, what *do* you think of her?" Babe appears in his robe.

"Whatever." Aaron lifts his cereal bowl from the table and pads out to the other room.

Eric stands in the middle of the kitchen in pajamas, his brother at his side, still groggy. "Can I eat breakfast in the family room, too?"

"Of course, honey," Lorena says. "Help Joshy with his."

Lorena and Allison silently start preparations for Thanksgiving dinner, leaving Babe with a cup of coffee and the financial section. Babe's mother and father are coming at three. His sister isn't coming. His sister, Lorena knows, has refused to speak to him for seven years, though he never says why; she despises him, that's all anyone knows. Babe makes glancing references to sibling rivalry.

Soon the television is blaring from the other room. Babe gets up and watches the boys from the doorway.

"Great," he says to Lorena, "your fat kid is my son's idol."

"Keep your voice down, Babe." Lorena tries not to laugh. "Don't be so mean."

After Babe goes up to shower, she and Allison wash and dress the turkey.

"Someone's in a foul mood," Allison says. She dumps three pounds of string beans into the sink.

"Allison." Lorena stands behind her. "There's something I want to ask you. There's something I need to know." Lorena holds her breath for a moment, wondering if her plan is sheer lunacy. "Do you feel it the way I do?"

The room goes silent with the humming in Lorena's ear.

"Do you feel something there?" She moves her hands up Allison's body, from hips to her chest, pressing approximately where her heart might be.

"Lorena." Her name in Allison's mouth is soft, pleasing, nearly indecipherable.

"Tell me." Lorena steps even closer, pressing herself against Allison's back.

Lorena tries to turn off her mind, which is buzzing out of control. What does she actually know about this girl, daughter of a minister, whose life is mapped out to exclude people like Babe and herself? And here is the joke, Lorena realizes, something Babe will never imagine: Allison could never end up with someone like him. Even the lure of his sexy nomadic life will not—cannot—derail the Bentley train of liberalism and honor. Allison is someone who will not even allow herself love when love comes to her, an adoring female professor, an employer, a fan. She will probably finish Smith with honors, then on to social work school. She'll end up married somewhere happily to a liberal do-gooder lawyer in a suburb somewhere near Manhattan.

Fresh-faced and flush, Allison stammers to answer.

Lorena presses against her now with purpose. "You hate rich people, don't you, Allison? I can see it on your face. You hate the way we sprawl in Connecticut, taking up space. I'm not one of them, Allison. But then again you hate women who love you, don't you? You hate yourself."

Allison backs away nervously. "I don't hate anyone, Lorena."

"No? Not even me?" Lorena whispers.

Before Allison can manage to answer, Josh Spencer appears in the kitchen. Rushing in socks, he slips, wind-milling his arms, gasping for air. The loud sound of his distress breaks Lorena's trance.

"What is it, Josh?" Lorena is annoyed at his scrawny body, at the way he moves stiff-legged like a robot. *Making it up,* she thinks. *He's making it up.* There isn't much time before Babe re-emerges, and Lorena needs an answer.

Josh has his hands at his neck, his small frame shuddering with the effort to breathe.

"Stop it, Josh," Lorena's voice is harsher than she intended. "I've had enough."

Josh heaves his body upward, his lips working a silent alphabet of airless vowels. Lorena rushes around the kitchen counter, grabbing him by the shoulders.

"Joshua Keith, stop this nonsense immediately!"

Eric and Aaron drift into the hallway with empty bowls of cereal.

"Joshy, please," Allison stands by Lorena's side, pleading. "You have our attention. What is it? What do you want? We love you, sweetheart. We love you."

The whole scene seems suddenly foolish to Lorena. The pained words the girl is speaking, the way Josh's thin lips are turning blue.

"Lorena," Allison says, perfectly in unison with her thoughts.

Lorena drops to her knees. "Josh?"

"Stop! Get away!" From the staircase, in bare feet, Babe rushes them, pushing Allison out of the way, his rage flushing his face. Lorena is afraid for everyone, for her marriage, for Joshy, who is sinking slowly to the floor.

Lorena tries to hold her husband back. "No, Babe."

He shoves her aside, grabbing the child who lies limply on the floor. Placing one hand firmly on his Josh's shoulder, he punches the center of the boy's belly. Lorena rushes to the middle of the gigantic stainless steel kitchen, then turns around. She's forgotten why she's there. Babe punches harder, and finally something round flies into the air from the back of Josh's throat.

Everyone takes a step back as it falls to the floor. Babe bends to pick it up.

"A grape." Babe shows it to Lorena. His face is red. "That's just perfect. You and those damn fruit baskets all over the house."

Joshy is coughing, curled in a ball at his father's knee, a string of slime on his chin. Babe lifts his son off the floor like a rag doll, hugging him to his chest.

"Why didn't you do anything?" He is looking directly at her. For a minute, she forgets Allison is there; she forgets everything, and concentrates.

"I don't know," she says.

"What did you think I was doing?" He pets the boy absently.

Like a door swinging open, something in Lorena unlatches. She feels it spread from her diaphragm up toward her throat.

"I never know what you're doing," she screams.

"What *I'm* doing?"

"Don't you dare! Don't you even dare. You think I'm stupid?" She thinks of the waiting room and the silent crying. "You think I'm blind?"

"My son could have choked to death, while you were…
what?" Babe says. "What was it you were doing, Lorena?"

Lorena lunges across the room, digging her fingers into
Allison's shoulders, as if once and for all she might actually
possess something, and kisses her desperately on the mouth.
The tips of the girl's teeth press unevenly into Lorena's lips,
bruising, resisting, biting back. When Lorena pulls away, the
girl is blank. *There*, she thinks, *isn't that what everyone wanted?*
She does not see the disbelief on Allison's face. Turning on her
heel, she faces Babe, who still holds a whimpering Josh in his
arms.

"You think you're the only one?" Lorena screams.

"How dare you act this way in front of my children." Babe's
voice booms through the room. Josh cringes, rolling his eyes up
at the ceiling.

"Me, in front of the children?" Lorena says.

"Don't you ever speak to me this way again." He gets up,
carrying Josh in his arms.

"You don't even love him!"

It surprises Lorena how quiet a scream can be. She thinks
about it long after Allison's bags are packed and she has quietly
instructed Aaron to drive the young woman to the train station.

How amazingly quiet.

Aaron must be the one, months later, who finds the letter
with its cancelled stamp, its Manhattan postmark. He finds it
during the tail end of summer, the year before his second try
at boarding school. Somehow she and Babe have managed to
work things out, stay together, navigating the dangerous shoal
of marriage. New babysitter. This time a man from Sweden,
named Sven, who has been with them ever since the au pair

disaster, as Lorena has come to think of the incident. A vaguely androgynous man with wide hips, whom Eric likes and Joshy loves. Even Aaron on his infrequent visits appreciates Sven. "At least you know he won't be balling the Ad Man."

The note is written in cramped blue ink, addressed to Babe in a woman's handwriting. It is unsigned and consists of a single sentence: "You never read a line of E.L. Doctorow in your life." Lorena finds it in her pocketbook, while noting the distinct absence of money from her wallet. Thirty bucks, which makes her know that Aaron is the culprit, for this is the summer of missing objects: earrings, coins, dollar bills, Babe's gold Rolex watch. She imagines throwing the note in the trash compactor, rather than showing it to Babe or raising a fuss, something she barely manages anymore. Why should the message be transmitted? She knows without a doubt who the author is, though she can't imagine exactly how Aaron might have intercepted it. The creamy stationery is living proof that some girls can withstand the pressure. Some girls get away and, from a distance, wise up. Not Lorena, though. She is living proof that some girls don't. The memory of the name, of saying it quietly to herself with the hope of conjuring up strength and passion, comes back to Lorena like an insect sting. She flattens the paper out on her thigh and carries it up to Babe's desk, where she signs the girl's name, in a similar blue cramped style. She wants to remember.

Allison Bentley, Lorena writes, slowing her pen to curl the tail of the *y*.

WONDERFUL
YOU

WONDERFUL YOU

ONE DESPERATE SUNDAY IN *Cien Fuegos* when Ricardo was a boy, his mother strangled Tita.

"We are the poor ones, *niño*," she said, stuffing and serving the hen for dinner.

The old bird had dropped many eggs into Ricardo's waiting hands, followed him down the dirt road nearly all the way to the school where the nuns used to preach about sin. Tita was discerning; she understood temptation. She waited all day at the side of the road while Ricardo sat in his chair in the little room with the red flag, where God had been replaced by a lady in a uniform, who repeated slogans about the government: *Until victory, always.*

Sometimes, out back during recess, Ricardo convinced Diego, Hector, or Pedro to play *Communista* with him. Ricardo played the wife, passionately kissing Diego, who was the husband, and then Pedro, the soldier turning Diego in for being a traitor to the Party. Some of the boys actually kissed him back; Ricardo's fervent belief in Cuba gave him a certain political appeal.

Mostly he kept to himself, though, glancing down the road and watching Tita's head bobbing for seeds, like an old nun pecking out prayers.

"Murderer," Ricardo told his mother.

He refused to allow her arms around him, knocking them off his shoulders when she tried to apologize. She set the table with special linen as the old *tias* took their seats, clapping when Patria and Libertad appeared on the staircase, twin brides in matching hand-sewn dresses of ribbon and silk.

"Patty and Libby only have one *quinceañera, niño*," Ricardo's mother whispered. "What was I supposed to do?"

The black market was fickle, even for families whose fathers worked directly for Party leaders. Ricardo's father had given everything up to join the inner circle, but he spent the better part of every month in Havana. Ricardo asked why they couldn't all live together.

"*Hijo*, you're safer here with *Mami's* family," his father said.

Wait until he heard about Tita.

Through dinner Ricardo cried quietly, refusing to eat from Tita's tender breast. His cries grew louder when the *tias* praised the presentation of an elaborate cake made with Tita's final eggs. The frosting said *Feliz Cumpleaños*.

"Don't cry, *hermano*," his sisters said in one voice. "*Papi* will buy you another chicken."

Ricardo didn't eat the lunch his mother made the next day in case she'd poisoned it: bread and cheese, a slice of birthday cake. He wanted the sweet taste of frosting on his tongue, but he couldn't forget what he'd seen the day before: his mother chasing Tita around the mango tree, her fingers snapping Tita's neck with a casual twist, Tita's limp body being carried to the kitchen for plucking. Ricardo shuddered. He'd heard stories of brother turning on brother, neighbor turning in neighbor, husband betraying wife. He thought the worst of everyone now, even himself.

"*Niño*," his mother said in the morning when he pushed away his *café y pan*, "kiss your *mami* goodbye." She was on her way downtown, where she worked as a clerk in a government office. Holding him close, she smelled so sweetly of perfume and lotion that he almost forgot his grudge.

At the door, she faced him. "Do you think I would let my darlings starve? We'll get another Tita for you, *mi amor.* You'll see." She lowered her voice, eyes twinkling. "Your father will march into Castro's henhouse and get you the best Communist chicken in the world."

Ricardo did not smile.

He did not bring up the pink-orange claw his mother had left next to his bed for him to find that morning, though he had it in his pocket. He did not even speak when she walked back across the room and stood by his chair to brush back his hair with her cool hand.

"I am sorry, *Ricardito.*"

On his way to school, Ricardo searched under every fence post and tree stump to find the perfect place to bury his dangerous lunch. He ripped it into pieces, even the cake, and covered it with leaves, checking over his shoulder for spies.

He planned to get Hector to wrestle him when he got to the school. In *La Revolución,* two boys were chosen to play Castro and Castro's brother, fighting for power over Cuba. Hector was not the best-looking choice. He had thick lips and a strange glow in his eyes that made him seem slow, but he was always willing to wrestle as the weaker brother, and he never seemed to mind when Ricardo pressed him to the mat, lips against neck, thigh in his groin.

The tour bus was leaving Barcelona at six a.m., and the American woman still wasn't on it. Late as usual, she'd had a bad habit of delaying their departures by at least fifteen minutes; Ricardo found it amusing. After blowing out the electricity in the *parador* this morning, she'd sent the maids scurrying out of their beds.

The very old man who ran the small hotel handed out candles from a sack, but before he'd limped back around with matches, the sun had risen. Ricardo put on a robe and stood in the doorway as the olive-skinned maids huddled elbow to elbow under a chipped archway crying *"Auxilio!"* as if the Spanish Empire were coming to an end, their nightgowns thin in the gray light of morning. Ricardo wondered if these were the old man's granddaughters and tried to call one over, but she blushed and turned away.

Ricardo had spent an entire summer in Europe already, a graduation gift from his father. He was used to the August heat, the idle chitchat of strangers whose faces ran together with paintings and photographs in a familiar blur. Spain was his last country—Barcelona the final stop, with several daylong junkets by bus to Valencia, Toledo, Sevilla, Madrid. Their very names held a kind of magic for him, as if somehow they formed a map of possibility, the final destinations of summer, his last chance.

The tour guide, a relentlessly cheerful European named Mercedes, looked at her watch. Like all the other tour guides of the summer, Mercedes had fleshy arms and a pungent smell of sweat mingling with her cologne.

"Buenas dias!" She nodded toward an empty seat, calling attention to American bad manners. "Shall we start the guide, even if we can't start the tour?" She began to reveal their day: Tejera Park, Los Burgos, and the Museo de Navarra.

The American woman finally arrived, offering a quick apology, and took the empty seat next to Ricardo. The other tourists, mostly Germans in tube socks, sent up a cheer as the bus sputtered forward. The American woman watched out the window, silent, and sad somehow; Ricardo was slightly put off by her fragile appearance. Reedy, almost. It reminded him of an article he'd read about birds and their small, hollow bones.

"Blow-drying my hair," she said. "I forgot to plug in the adapter and almost burned the place down."

The young man seated next to her was barely eighteen, Violet guessed. He looked a bit like the figure in an El Greco painting they would likely see in Toledo—Saint Martin and the Beggar— long, gaunt body, close-cropped hair. *Young enough to be my son.* Something about his soft pink lips and clear eyes made him seem foreign, though she couldn't discern an accent in his impeccable Castilian—better than hers, and she had taught Spanish for sixteen years at Montclair Community College. *Canadian*, she decided, pressing at her skirt as it billowed in the heat.

She had been touring Europe since May.

The young man stopped writing in a notebook to scratch his chin with the pencil. A slight beard had grown in overnight, rugged. She studied his green eyes—the color of ivy—and the curve of his neck under the thin shirt, tucked into the same tan corduroys as yesterday. Leather sandals, a shoulder bag in his lap.

Not American, anyway.

Looking out at the Catalonian countryside, Violet thought how Edward would have loved to see the old gypsies hanging their wash over the stone wall at the edge of the city. He would have made up a line of poetry about how they looked like old crows, so worn in their black widow dresses. But Edward was not in Barcelona; he was home in New Jersey, making decisions about their life.

Violet's sister tried not to gloat. "Imagine," Judith said, "Your Edward, a mere human after all! He's practically searching for his mother."

"Aren't we all?" said Violet.

Still, the thought yielded a terrifying sensation, more like strangulation than sorrow. She found a recurrent difficulty filling her lungs with air had become socially embarrassing. Once, she nearly fainted in the faculty lounge.

"Panic attacks," Judith said, offering the name of a shrink, who insisted on downplaying the dramatics and yet still using words that packed a wallop.

Anger, the shrink said, *fear*.

The tour group split up in Pamplona after they'd tackled the major sights. The bus driver pointed the Germans to the center of town, staying behind and flipping through a magazine while Mercedes napped.

Ricardo wandered aimlessly into the warm afternoon.

He found the American woman lunching at an outdoor café.

"Last month, in Romania," he said with his best grammar, "I caused the blackout of an entire village with my electric razor."

She squinted the sun out of her eyes, motioning for him to sit in an empty wrought-iron chair at her table.

"How did you know I spoke Spanish?" she said.

Ricardo pointed south toward Barcelona: "I heard you speaking to the old man back at the hotel."

"Your Castilian is perfect. Where are you from?"

"Cuba." He shook her hand: "Ricardo."

"Violet," she said. "Havana?"

"*Cien Fuegos*, but I live in New York now."

She looked surprised.

"My mother was Cuban," Ricardo said. "After she died, my father got us out."

"I teach Cuba as an example of Spanish colonization, failed political vision, and cultural despair," Violet said. "Perhaps that's insensitive of me."

"It's okay," Ricardo said. "My sisters still live there. They think it's wonderful. Patty is going to medical school, and Libby raises chickens. My mother named them after a Party slogan: *Patria y Libertad*."

She nodded. "Patriotism and Freedom. It's prettier in Spanish."

"We always sent them American money in the mail. There's a trick to it: You lay the bills flat between the pages of a poetry book to fool the officials. Or so we hoped. When my mother died and my father took me out, they were put under surveillance. We used to get letters with some of the words blacked out."

"It's like letting go of everything when your mother dies." Her voice was mournful. "My mother died right before this trip."

"I was very young," Ricardo said. "My mother died in a bus accident. My *tias* say she was carrying a bomb in her purse meant for *El Caballero*, but my father says that's nonsense."

"What do you think?"

Ricardo shrugged. "She could have been working for Castro or working against him. I don't know."

Violet's hair curled in the heat as if it might lift off her head.

"Are you traveling alone?"

"I was supposed to stay with relatives in Avila, but it didn't work out," he said. "I couldn't find my mother's family." Their conversation paused. "I'm going to the University of Madrid for graduate school in the fall."

"To study more Spanish?"

Ricardo shook his head. "Architecture."

She fingered some postcards, looking at the writing as she waved them back and forth. "They're for my students."

He dug around his shoulder bag and found some stamps, offering them up. He pointed at her neat signature. "It's a lovely name: Violet Fields."

"I keep meaning to take back my maiden name." Her face was pink. "You don't seem like an architect type." She stared over his shoulder, as if it hurt to look him in the eye.

His father had already paid his tuition at Madrid, Ricardo thought. When Violet insisted on paying for his drink, Ricardo told her a secret.

"What I really want to be," he said, "is an artist."

After the bus crash that killed Ricardito's mother, he grew up quickly. At first his father lay around the house in his underwear, drinking rum from the bottle, which Patty or Libby tried to hide out back in the garden. When Ricardo turned nine, there were secret meetings in the backyard, whispered accusations, neighbors' disapproving glances.

His father sent him off to bed with a pat on the back and a wink. "Now we're going to get somewhere, *hijo*. You'll see."

Beware political dissent, the school janitor hissed, cornering him in the hallway. *What do you think killed your mother?*

"*Papi*," the twins warned, "we have Ricardito to think of. We have our future."

The year Ricardo turned ten, his father woke him out of a sound sleep and carried him to a beat-up car, then to a rickety boat, and finally to what must have been the tiniest airplane in the world. His father carried him up the ladder and belted him in the seat. The whole ride to Miami Ricardo's ears popped; his head buzzed. His father slept through the thunderstorm that rocked the little plane, but Ricardo threw up twice: once in the well where his legs were and once in his own lap.

There hadn't been time to pack clothes or even a photograph of his mother or sisters. No toys or shoes, though later his father would present him with a box of things from Cuba. In the pocket of his jacket, Ricardo gripped his only worldly possessions: three Cuban coins, a marble, and Tita's dried-out chicken claw from his mother. Flying in the tiny airplane, looking down at the lights and the small disappearing island, he didn't know he would never see his sisters again, or *Cien Fuegos*, his mother's home.

Violet watched a deep orange sun sinking behind the red rooftops as the Alta Vista bus slid along under a wide Spanish sky. Turning to Ricardo, she thought she saw tears in his eyes, but as the bus reached the great, embattled entranceway, Ricardo yawned and smiled.

She'd been mistaken. She was alone. "I'm nobody's mother."

Ricardo raised his eyebrows, soft pink lips parting as if to speak.

After a belabored effort to park behind the little *parador*, the bus finally rolled to a stop. Violet handed Ricardo an email printout: Dearest, Please call. We Need to talk. Georgia is ready to get married. Hope you're having fun! Love, Edward.

*

The Germans filed off, inviting Mercedes for a nightcap at the café across the street. In France and Italy, Violet had learned to appreciate their constant tobacco smiles, their enthusiasm for Europe, which seemed like something to count on.

Ricardo held the email. "Edward?"

"My husband," Violet said. She had stuffed the notice in her purse the previous day.

"I'm sorry."

"Funny," she said. "I felt like crying, all day, and then I thought…"

He tilted his head, waiting for the rest of the sentence. By the look on his face, Violet realized she'd made a mistake.

She motioned to the empty aisle. "I think it's time to go."

Six on the dot the next morning, when Violet appeared, the Germans gave her a standing ovation. Violet took a deep bow. This was a three-day excursion to the South—Toledo, Sevilla, and Madrid.

"You're almost on time!" Mercedes said, as Violet made her way down the bus's rubber aisle to her usual seat.

"Sleep well?" she asked Ricardo.

The night before he'd spent hours at the outside café across the street. "I'm hung over."

Violet cleared her throat. "Alcohol!"

"To watch the Germans, you'd have thought it was water."

"I tossed and turned all night," she said, "I could hear you all the way across the street, explaining to everyone how I'm not your mother."

He blushed. "What do Germans know?"

"Well, they're right," Violet said. "And without him, I'm a spinster."

"Edward?"

"I did meet a man in France."

Ricardo felt his excitement rise. "A man?"

"A wonderful man!"

"At your hotel?"

Violet patted the thin material of her skirt: "No."

"You went out?"

"To a disco."

Mercedes began to speak into a microphone. She was wearing a yellow straw hat and seemed in particularly good humor. "Today we are starting our three-day tour, featuring Madrid: city of industry, fashion, and broken hearts." The bus driver popped in a video of the sites they would see: the *Palacio Real*, the *Plaza Mayor, Puerta del Sol*.

"You went to a disco?" Ricardo's voice floated above the sound of the Germans' dull drone.

"One night when I couldn't sleep, I went for a walk and found the most delicious little dance club." She caught her breath, excited by the memory. "It was so hot that night, Bastille Day, and I stepped inside because I knew it would be nice and cool."

"Was he French?" The skin on Ricardo's arms prickled, as if the stifling air might actually burn him.

"He was from San Diego," she said. "A divorcé."

"An American," Ricardo whispered. How many times had he himself dreamed of falling in love with a dark handsome stranger from a dark land? A divorcé from San Diego would do, anyone, as long as it was someone belonging to Ricardo, even if only for the night. Suddenly Ricardo wanted to kiss Violet Fields in a dark smoky disco with throbbing music in his ears while men from every nation looked on, wanting him.

Violet peered through the window at the low-growing

trees that slid along the countryside. He followed her gaze, dreaming, seeing that some were gnarled and dense, others shady and expansive, with branches like feathers.

The next few days, Ricardo felt sullen. He thought about writing his father the truth: that he wanted to go to Paris and study with artists. Day after day on the bus, he'd start out listening to Mercedes' chatter but soon be lost in the hot yellow sun of his own yearning, imagining he was walking and talking with Violet.

As morning developed into sweltering afternoon, the driver hummed to himself, nodding as he drove. Cool air blasted from the vents, lulling even Mercedes to sleep; Violet seemed half in a trance. Ricardo said her name.

She turned. He hesitated. "What is it?"

"Did you kiss that man?"

She laughed and patted his leg. "What kind of a question is that?"

He leaned his head on the seat in front of him. "Did you kiss that man from California?"

She lightly swatted him, as if he weren't serious, then sat back and closed her eyes. "He kissed me, not that it's any business of yours."

Ricardo studied the way her hair framed her face, the freckles on her neck. She seemed to grow younger the longer he knew her. "I see."

"What do you see?" Violet said sharply. "Because frankly I think you're too young to see anything." She was glaring. "How old are you, Ricardo?"

"Twenty-five." It would be true in a few months.

"What does a person actually see at your age?"

The question seemed to startle her, giving him hope. "I see a country," he leaned over her to look out the window. "A beautiful country."

At lunch in Segovia, Violet announced to everyone—even the Germans—that she intended to drink all the wine in Spain. Ricardo tried to keep her glass filled, but she sipped slowly. He said, "What about you, Violet?"

She skewered a shrimp. "What about me?"

"That's just it, isn't it?" He leaned across the table. "No one knows a thing about you. I mean, I'm going to be an architect; the Germans are always going to be German, and Mercedes, here, is very soon going to be free of us."

Mercedes laughed, touching his arm.

"So, Violet, what are you going to be?"

"When I grow old?" she teased.

"Whenever."

"No clue." She raised her glass. "Except maybe alone." He barely heard her above the din of the restaurant. The Germans were embroiled in an animated discussion.

"Speak in Spanish," Mercedes pleaded. She'd been talking all day into the bus microphone as they drove past cathedrals of stone and great ivory crosses carved into cliffside cemeteries, everything yellow in southern Europe in the summer. "Even my brain is dry," she said.

Violet patted her arm. "*Claro, querida.*" Of course.

Ricardo sat back, watching the Germans at the end of the table. They now seemed to be singing English nursery rhymes.

Violet hummed along. After traveling so long with a group even the most unpredictable behavior had come to feel expected. At that moment anything seemed possible: She might return to the *parador* with the fountain out front in Barcelona and whisper to Ricardo's sleeping profile, "I'll never see that wonderful man again."

Or you.

Wonderful you.

At noon, on their last day in Spain, the bull ring at *Les Arenes* was crowded with men in rolled-up shirtsleeves, abandoning their wives and children to the higher seats *en el sombre*, the shade, by climbing down the stone steps to the bull pens for a closer look. Even Violet seemed slightly drunk with excitement. She sat in front of Ricardo, below him for once. He enjoyed the top of her head, the clasp of a pearl necklace, her bare shoulders. She wore a large-brimmed sombrero.

"Last day blues?" he asked her.

Violet nodded. "Back to school next week."

The night before, they'd all thrown themselves an impromptu farewell party, joking about the trouble they might get into without Mercedes on Saturday, her day off. Even the Germans were subdued, cowed by the heat and chafing against the quiet.

"I know I look ridiculous," Violet said, indicating her hat.

"You look pretty," he said.

When the bull finally appeared—furious and muscular, kicking up orange dust and huffing through large black nostrils—Ricardo watched, hypnotized, from his perch safely high up near the stone coliseum's pinnacle. The day was suffused with colors, peanut shells, the smells of urine and *cerveza*. He felt hypnotized by the beauty of *el toro*, the lusty tone of his hide, the sheen of his muscles. When the horse-backed *picadores* appeared in full uniform, Violet leaned her whole body back against Ricardo's knees.

The sensation of her spine against his shin was so exciting it took a full minute for him to realize what was happening. Violet had fainted.

As she slipped to the hot stone at their feet, Ricardo grabbed under each of her arms, but before he could lift her, Gustav—a big, blonde, oafish German—took over and was carrying her, groggy and silent, to the bus.

Ricardo trailed behind, holding Violet's hat.

Once she was laid out flat on the bus's back seat, Ricardo insisted Gustav return to the fight. Splashing water from a cooler on Violet's forehead, he fanned her with a program. He opened the button of her collar, imagining what it might be like to touch her.

"Water," she said.

He hovered, trying to shake off his shame at the desire he'd felt. "Don't get up."

Violet was looking at him, her eyes working to focus. He leaned down and kissed her. She came to life, opening her mouth to deepen the kiss, then pushed him away.

"How humiliating," she said.

Once Violet had recovered, the group gathered for some final sightseeing in *Las Ramblas*, the old part of town. Ricardo watched the crowds in the market, losing track of the others. He'd read once that *Mario Vargas Llosa* said no other city in the world was as snobbish as Barcelona, except Milan, but when he looked into the Spaniards' eyes, he found the glancing reflection of his dead mother staring back.

At dinner, the Germans replayed the bullfight for Violet, making finger horns and dancing around the table as the mariachi serenaded. "You missed the best part!" Gustav said, pretending to be a bull about to meet the sword.

Violet protested slightly.

Heading to the bus that would take them the short distance to the hotel for their final night, Violet took Ricardo's arm. As they approached a mailbox, Ricardo searched his bag for the postcards he'd composed the night before: the stone statue for Patty and Libby; the severed ears of defeated bulls addressed to New York City.

"For my father," he said, showing them to Violet.

The letter he'd written about art and life and his secret desires was safely tucked in the pocket of his linen jacket.

As the bus rode toward the *parador* for the last time, Ricardo waited for another of Violet's confessions. "What are you thinking?"

She turned toward him. "Oh, about Edward."

The Germans were singing a patriotic song. Ricardo was about to speak when she placed a hand on his arm.

"It wasn't the thought of the blood that made me faint," she said.

He felt the warmth of her skin through his shirt, and closed his eyes. He fingered the letter to his father. "What then?"

The bus lurched forward, bucking slightly against ancient cobblestones.

"It was their lives," Violet said, "their sad, caged lives."

Ricardo suddenly saw the arc of his own oncoming life, the paintings he'd make, the women who'd adore him, and the beautiful men he would love.

He reached out into the dark for Violet's hand.

WHAT'S
NOT
MY FAULT?

WHAT'S NOT MY FAULT?

LILY AND JANET SAT on the bed, memorizing what they could of Mary-Kay, who, after so many surgeries and treatments and relapses, was now dying.

She seemed nothing at all like the woman who'd given them life.

Time threaded apart, quick yet absurdly slow. Weeks of the same slack jaw, same fever, no movement whatsoever; so that even hoping for something—progress in either direction—seemed cruel.

They might as well still have been little girls, perched on the bed, waiting for their mother to wake and make them breakfast or take them swimming. They sat on the bottom half of a pilly hospice blanket.

They were all grown up, but presiding over their mother's dying body, it didn't feel that way.

"What about a priest?" Lily finally said. "Maybe Mother would want one?"

"Mrs. Robinson," Janet said loudly into her mother's ear. "Do you want a priest?"

It took most of Mary-Kay's energy to reach the surface of consciousness, but she managed to wave off the suggestion. She wanted nothing of religion. Not any more.

She made the gesture again, bony arm barely lifting off the

bed, fingers flicked decisively and suspended in air.

How lovely. Communication with her daughters should always have been so clear, so well executed.

"Take it easy, Mrs. Robinson," Janet said, still very loud. "It's not your fault."

Mary-Kay hadn't spoken for days. The sound of her voice, strained and sickly, came as a surprise. "Well, of course it's not."

Janet touched her sister's arm, as if in the act of reaching out for their mother she'd somehow missed the mark. "It's okay. We're here."

"Yes, here," Mary-Kay said or maybe thought. "But it's not going very well, is it?"

Lily jumped to her feet. "Should we call for the doctor?"

These revivals were alarming. They'd been warned that the process of dying was anything but linear, and still it seemed all wrong.

Some people get very lucid just before they go, Dr. Alberts had said.

Janet hated his euphemisms: *just before they go*.

Go where?

Lily, by contrast, hated everything but these comforting bits of wisdom from the doctors. There was so much to hate over these past several years: the slow decline, the hushed conversations, the way her mother's wardrobe underwent a metamorphosis. Bulky gold amulets, jaunty knit slack suits—usually navy blue or lime green—and something like soft leather hiking boots.

Who but their mother would treat cancer as an excuse for a makeover?

She had acted exactly as if hysterectomies and colostomies and radiation were minor inconveniences. Even as recently as the last recurrence, she insisted on being dropped off at her chemotherapy treatments.

"Wait in the car," she said, as if she were running into the deli to get a loaf of bread. "It'll just take a few minutes."

Now, Mary-Kay flapped her eyes at the ceiling.

"What should we do?" Lily looked around, frightened. She was about to enter her second trimester with twins; it had taken her so many years and so much money to finally achieve a viable pregnancy that even the smallest thing exhausted her.

"It's just a weird little burst of energy," Janet said.

Mary-Kay's voice was like fine grade sandpaper. "Why is everyone yelling?"

"Extremes," Janet said in a normal voice. "It's what we Robinsons have come to."

Later, when they'd all gone home for the night, Mary-Kay thought it over. Her family came often, stayed late, said little.

And here it was, unexpectedly, a moment alone.

"Wait—what's not my fault?" she said aloud.

She was thinking about the fact that once she had loved another man as much as, if not more than, she loved Richard.

The night nurse sighed deeply and took Mary-Kay's temperature. "None of it is your fault, dear. Really, not a thing."

Lily didn't want the babies' names to rhyme.

"Of course not, sweetheart," her father said. He was taking her to an emergency obstetrician appointment. "Why would you?"

Outside the weather was mild, Indian summer. *Good for business,* Lily's husband always said.

Paul LeChance Construction did its best work in dry weather.

Paul wanted to work as much as possible, so he could be

around when the twins were born. Lily felt bad about asking her father to take her, especially now that her mother's cancer had recurred. But there was bleeding, and the appointment was early in the day.

"A couple of stitches to the cervix," the obstetrician had said cheerfully, "and those babies will stay right in place!"

Lily's father seemed pale and tired, seated across from the model of matching fetuses.

In the car, Lily said, "Daddy, they're going to sew me up like a sack of flour."

He patted her hand. "Don't worry, princess. Everything will be fine."

Lily could feel the babies moving under her ribs like heartburn wearing tennis shoes. She missed being thin and light on her feet. Missed her elastic figure and the appearance of youth, though she was thirty-seven and beginning to wrinkle around the eyes. She missed spin class and making love with Paul on Saturday morning, because now she was too nervous. Her skin felt tight as football leather: *If you touch me I'll pop.* It was her new favorite phrase, even when no one was around.

Her father turned expertly against traffic into the hospital lot. He pulled into a parking spot several yards from the entrance. "Put the seat back and lie flat. I just want to check on your mother and then I'll take you home."

"I'm starving," Lily said.

"Cafeteria?" her father said. "One toasted cheese and chocolate shake coming up!"

Lily watched her father cross the neat black pavement, heading toward Emergency, a short cut Janet had discovered after their mother's third surgery, when they sewed her back up without even attempting to remove any tumors. When Lily's father was a safe distance, Lily took out her Marlboro Lights and a can of Lysol. It was a soft day late in September, unusually pleasant. The parking lot was surprisingly busy.

Opening the car door wide, Lily lit a cigarette and inhaled deeply. On the ninth floor of the mammoth brick building, her mother was recovering from her final surgery. They would give her radiation to shrink the tumors and make her feel as comfortable as possible. This had given her sister a reason to pull herself together and Janet and their mother another excuse to gang up on Lily. Not to mention the fact that her dying all but obliterated the otherwise happy news of the twins. Her mother had always wanted grandbabies.

Lily always got the short end of the stick. When their mother carried on like a teenager with the junior high school principal, she was employed to act as cover, at the tender age of twelve, bribed with secret ice-cream sundaes and long afternoons at the movie or mall. The subterfuge turned Lily bitter at an early age. When things went downhill with Principal Howe, and their mother was secretly broken-hearted, she comforted her mother and kept it all under wraps, so Daddy wouldn't find out.

Janet had gotten to escape the entire mess by being a moody teenager, a normal high school girl with love interests of her own and friends who drove cars that could take her away.

Even when they were grown, when Janet suffered from nervous exhaustion after her divorce, sleeping on Mother's sofa and heading straight for a breakdown, who suggested she see a shrink, someone unrelated entirely to Janet's ex, a man she married after years of seeing him as an analyst? When Janet ran around the house, straightening the bedspreads and aligning the fringe on Mother's throw rugs, did Lily ever say *I told you so*? No, she kindly suggested medication. But did they ever offer *her* constructive criticism or a helping hand?

And now her mother's death was exactly coinciding with Lily's first happy moment: her long-awaited double miracles.

She really couldn't catch a break.

Pregnancy was worse than expected. The stress and gas made Lily feel like drinking again. Not real drinking, like when she was in college and used to wake up with naked people she didn't even know: cab drivers, professors, and once a woman from town. And not like after college, when she used to drive the car to Connecticut and wake up in jail. This was different; she longed for the pleasure of a lovely red wine, something mellow to calm the nerves. A glass of merlot would be good. She'd heard the Australians had perfected the art sometime after she'd gotten sober. Paul would worry, so she wouldn't tell him—they'd met in AA, a fact Lily downplayed around her family. Imagining the conversation:

"Lily and Paul go to AA together, Richard." Her mother, all whispery and conspiratorial. "You know, Alcoholics Anonymous."

"I'll drink to that!" Her father, lifting his scotch glass cheerfully.

Her mother, bemused: "Alcoholics don't have a sense of humor, darling. Let's just keep your little joke entrez nous."

Lily pictured her mother conjuring up all sorts of terrible images: a smoky little circle of greasy alcoholics in the basement of the local church, confession about a lousy childhood, a lousy life. Her mother had managed to twist Lily's teenage drinking into an accusation, like proof of early neglect or emotional abuse. Anyway, she wasn't really going to drink, and no one knew about the smoking.

Paul wanted to make it legal: "I think the twins should have parents who are *married*."

The generic reference to their babies as "the twins" irked her. "*Loving* parents are all any human being needs."

Lily stepped outside the car, although the doctor had told

her not to stand unless necessary. "They might just fall right out of there," the nurse had joked in a way Lily didn't appreciate. She stubbed out her cigarette on her father's tire, then flicked the nub across a Subaru wagon to her left, not seeing the driver approaching carrying a purse the size of a suitcase.

"Oh sorry," Lily said.

The woman gave her a dirty look.

"What, you've never seen somebody expecting twins?" She sprayed Lysol near her father's car.

The woman, who was small and was younger than Lily, trembled. "It's cruel, you know. Some people would give anything."

Some people. Lily slammed the car door, feeling guilty.

When Mary-Kay woke it was dark.

Richard was sitting by the bed, reading aloud from the paper.

Leave it to Richard to think of the *New York Times* at a moment like this, yet as she floated in and out of wars and crimes, political scandals—bridal announcements!—she was happy to know there were people around to carry on.

It was a bit of a surprise that she kept wondering about God.

But Mary Kay hadn't wanted God while giving birth to her girls or going through the battering ram of everyday life. She wouldn't need him now. And who was to say who or what God was? Maybe she was God. Or Gerald Howe, principal at Westchester Middle School. Maybe God was the only man she'd ever desired with every inch of her maturing body.

Making love on the living room sofa, they were caught in the act one afternoon by Lily, at the time a mere child disguised as a budding teenager. Maybe God was the look of awe and disgust on her face.

Or the pain Mary-Kay felt when Gerald broke things off.

Or maybe God is Richard, the patience and loyalty of a humble man. Mary-Kay listened to him drone on about the stock market. The delicate shape of his skull showed through his thinning hair; his nostril hairs stirred as he dozed off at the end of a paragraph on Internet companies. His ears protruded comically, wrinkling slightly at the lobe. She knew those ears better than she knew herself. Maybe God was that exact feeling of knowing.

As Mary-Kay tried to fend off the undertow of morphine, a memory floated up: a phone message playing quietly, somewhere after her second round of chemo, Lily's voice: *Not your little girl anymore, Daddy.*

"Hell of a way to announce the future," Mary-Kay had said, standing by the answering machine.

"She's eloping?" Richard looked stunned. He replayed the message twice more. Lily was running off to marry Paul. No one in the family was invited.

In those days Mary-Kay could clock the hours before she started feeling ill; she still had a little more time. "I suppose a private affair is better in her condition."

"We're really not invited?" Richard paced the room, mulling the insult, then sighed. "At least we'll save a bundle."

Mary-Kay patted his back. "That's the spirit, dear."

Now, she lay in a hospital bed dreaming of Gerald Howe, who'd broken things off so completely twenty-five years ago that it still took her breath away to call up the pain he had caused her. She remembered their last phone conversation: *Darling, did you really think we could go on like this forever?*

Yes, she'd said. *Why not? No one ever has to know.*

Lying did not come easily to him; he'd taken a vow. And so had she. Didn't they both have children and marriages to protect?

If anyone could pull it off, we can, she had said.

Good-bye, darling, he'd whispered. *Don't call here again.*

In her most recent dream, Gerald arrived for lunch, as if no years had passed.

How could she sit in a restaurant with Gerald Howe with tumors spreading like beach pebbles along the banks of her colon, her gut, and her pancreas? Could she order wine and laugh about the good old days, which—now that she'd had some years to think about it—might not have been so good after all?

In the dream, she carried on gracefully, ordering chicken piccata, smiling over a white tablecloth and china plates.

Wearing a black tuxedo, Lily brought their meal, which Mary-Kay ate with gusto. The plate held two small pieces of chicken stuffed inside two tiny wooden boxes shaped like little coffins.

The aids came by to make Mary-Kay choke down a few driblets of applesauce and mashed potato, measuring every drop that went in and came out.

Later, Mary-Kay brought up the soft substance in a mess on her gown.

She suddenly remembered her father, now long dead.

Once he'd taken her ice skating—she could see him kneeling at the foot of the bed to help her tie up her boots, a grown woman wearing Peggy Flemming powder-pink skates.

Her father cared very little for her; that's what she should remember.

The present, not the past; that's what she should catalog. She tore the IV out of her arm and threw it in the air.

"Now, now, dear," said the private day nurse Richard had hired, who had little patience for disturbances.

"Yes," Mary-Kay screamed. "Now! Now!"

"We know, Mrs. Robinson," Janet said. "No one likes this part very much."

Janet had taken to making grand pronouncements over hurried dinners of Chinese take-out. *I don't think Mrs. Robinson would want anyone giving up.* And, *We really ought to take turns rubbing her back and holding her feet.* Mary-Kay couldn't help being proud, even of Janet's quirks. Who thinks of calling her own mother Mrs. Robinson in the fifth grade?

Janet had come a long way since the divorce and her most recent nervous breakdown.

The insult wasn't the cancer, or treatments, futile radiation, failed surgery, Mary-Kay thought. It was a lazy mind producing some sentimentalized idea about what was happening. *(Is this happening? Oh my God! Oh, God, please help me!)*

What was the experience of dying minus the violins?

"What do you think it means, Daddy?" Lily said, watching her mother grimace.

"I think she's smiling," Paul said.

Lily leaned her head on Paul's shoulder. He was so gentle, even when he was wrong. "Do you know what the last thing my mother said to me was?"

She leaned in, smelled the familiar fragrance of his hair: sweat and soap. "*Love hard, baby.*"

"Love's hard?"

"It was a command."

Janet checked the morphine drip.

"What are you two whispering about?"

There lay their mother, completely unembellished and bald. She seemed to disappear into the white hospital sheets. There was a certain comfort in having the moment finally arrive. During the last months, Lily had hated how normal it all seemed, how misleading. No more refusing to let anyone come in and sit with her during the treatments. He mother sat fully dressed and chatted with the nurse as if she were getting her nails done. Her mother had known everyone there by name and diagnosis. Tuesday had been her regular treatment day. (Today was Tuesday, Lily realized.)

A year ago, Janet and Lily trailed her through the waiting room that last time, each with a cup of chocolatey coffee from Starbucks.

Behind a white curtain, Mary-Kay motioned to the cup of coffee in Lily's hand. "That stuff's going to kill you." Before Lily got a chance to pretend it was decaf, Janet motioned to the clear bag hanging on a silver post above Mary-Kay's head. "Ditto, Mrs. R."

Mary-Kay smiled. "You always were the witty one."

"I'm serious. Why don't you try something alternative: acupuncture or Chinese herbs? That stuff's going to kill you before it stops any tumors."

"This is just the Benadryl," Mary-Kay said. "The toxic stuff comes next."

Janet felt her mother's arm. "It's so cold."

Everyone at the treatment center loved Mary-Kay, praising her for being brave, for remaining in the fight against all odds. The other patients stopped in behind Mary-Kay's curtain, patting Lily and lighting up at the mention of twins, as if the treatment room were one big family den. *Cancer reunion, where some relatives died chatting about weather.*

The only proof of reality was the tube dripping poison into her mother's arm. Sometimes she just wanted the whole thing to end.

Do something, hold her hand, tell her a secret—anything!

"Paul wants to name the babies Daniel and Annabel," she finally managed.

"Danny and Annie?" Mary-Kay snorted.

Janet looked alarmed. "Don't do that horrible rhyming thing, Lily. You'll totally regret it."

"Do you have any ideas?"

"Well now, let's see," Mary-Kay said.

Lily cleared her throat in the silence.

Janet sighed. Mary-Kay leaned forward, patting Janet's hand. "Buck up, sweetheart. All men are shits."

"You might have mentioned that earlier. Like before I got married."

"Never too late to become a lesbian, dear."

A passing nurse chuckled.

"You don't mean Daddy, though, do you?" Lily was suddenly panicked. "Daddy's not a shit."

"No, no, not Daddy," Janet and Mary-Kay said.

"Of course, Daddy is a little absent at times," Mary-Kay said.

"Yeah," Janet said. "Like when you really need him."

Lily's eyes filled with tears: pregnancy hormones.

Then someone else stepped behind the white curtain to deliver the bad news.

*

After several days, as the hospice tech came to thread tubes down Mary-Kay's throat, she realized that dying was like living but with fewer obligations. Death was like life but without banking, dishes, and radio stations. *No Q-tips.* No terrorism or auto insurance payments.

"Is she trying to say something?" Janet asked.

"Maybe we should take our dinner out to the hall?" Lily, ever timid.

"Nonsense," said Richard. The only word he'd spoken all day.

Richard thought all this was somehow his fault, Mary-Kay knew. This afternoon he'd ordered another day on the feeding tube, an act of love, even if he couldn't figure out how to let go.

He was only now just catching up with her, a race he'd been losing since they'd had the children.

A part of her wished she could confess her sins and be forgiven.

All these years, standing at her side so solidly, Richard really might be wonderful. Maybe she did understand *something* about love, finally. Love and pain—and the space in between— Richard and Lily, Janet, and Gerald Howe.

Mary-Kay's family gathered around the bed trying to read her lips.

"It must be important," Lily said.

"She's saying she loves her family," Paul said. He held Lily's wrist, a carton of broccoli with garlic sauce in his other hand. "Maybe she wants you all to know."

"That's not it," Lily said softly. "Not our mother."

"Lily's right," Janet said. "Daddy, I think she's saying your name."

Richard stood: "It's okay, darling. I'm here."

"No, wait," Janet said, "it looks like something else."

Even diminished, Mary-Kay commanded them: They could feel her desire to communicate, see it in the way she thrashed her head. Her hand stayed in the air for no apparent reason, pinky slightly extended.

She was still raw, still sexy, even in death. Anyone could see it.

She shifted in the bed, opening her eyes suddenly.

God! The thought came against her will, but it was right, the only thing she had before her now. *Please. Yes. Please.*

Janet was still clutching a pair of plastic chopsticks. Paul still glancing down at the Chinese food.

Lily watched as Mary-Kay's mouth opened and closed, parched and searching, lips puckering noisily, once and again, as if she were blowing her final kisses good-bye.

MARRY

ME

QUICKLY

THROUGH THE WINDOW WILL can see the little crowd of smokers on the doorstep. Each wears a watered-down version of his fiancé's face.

When he opens the door, they startle collectively like a flock of geese.

One of them says, "We were starting to think the bell was broken."

Stammering, Will points behind him. "We're just in the middle…"

The youngest smoker pushes a cloud through her nose, her hair a parade of yellow curls. Will should step aside and let them in. For some reason he is unable to.

"I'm Wilhelm…Will." In his bowtie and boutonniere, who else could he be? "I'm Andy's…"

The blonde interrupts: "Yeah, we know. I'm his sister. This is our mother, Rusty."

Rusty is nervous and quick, a fragile bird. She steps forward to crush out her cigarette on the face of the mail slot, where Will has recently spelled out his and Andy's new last name in gold sticky letters: Wojak-Livingston.

Rusty points behind her. "That over there is Marion Carroll."

Will nods at the old man in the brown fedora, who waves

a pipe, wafting a stream of cherry-flavored air.

Rusty adds: "He needs to use the john."

She seems to blow into the house through front door, making Will wonder just how easy it would be to shoo her back out.

"The head?" Marion Carroll says. "If you don't mind."

Will turns toward the back of the house, where all the guests are waiting, where the ceremony has begun. Andy's sister hauls a long, rectangular package inside with her. He tries to step out of her way, but his soon-to-be-husband's eyes stare out of her pasty face, unnerving him.

"This is a gift," she says. "A *wedding* gift."

He can't discern if her tone is irony, mockery, or something else.

She prods: "So…Marion would like to use the facilities."

"Yes, of course."

Will shows the strange skinny man to the bathroom, politely pointing at the elegant silver paper towels.

"I'm very grateful for the kindness," Marion Carroll says. "And I hear congratulations are in order."

"Yes," Will says. "Any time. You're welcome."

Back in the foyer, Andy appears, looking like the handsome groom he is, in the beautiful dove-grey designer suit Will helped him pick.

"What's going on?" Andy stops cold when he sees the late arrivals.

The sister steps back as his mother rushes forward, a small unpleasant breeze. "Andy!"

From the hall, Will can see the minister check her watch. *This is my wedding day*, he thinks. Andy lifts his mother off the ground in an enthusiastic hug, then starts to apologize before she's even opened her mouth. "We waited as long as we could,

Ma. The minister has another ceremony to get to."

"Oh, Andy, what a wonderful house!" she says. "Just like you described."

Marion Carroll flushes the toilet and reappears. Andy looks at Will, mouthing, *Who's this?*

Will shrugs.

Rusty explains, "*This* is who drove us here. A kind stranger who didn't leave us stranded on the roadside."

"But what about Bo and Ginny?" Andy says. "I thought they were coming."

Will runs through a file of family names, the ones he's heard about for years now, trying to pinpoint first Marion Carroll, then Bo, then Ginny, until it all comes back. Ginny is the missing sister, the one in the middle, the one Andy loves best. Bo is the missing husband of the missing sister, the favored brother-in-law, who paid for Andy's college.

"Yes, where *are* Bo and Ginny?" Will asks, proud of his memory.

From the hallway: "They couldn't make it."

"Alice-James," Andy calls his sister out of the shadows. "Look at you!"

Will eyes the large blonde woman, wondering what he's supposed to see.

Will paces the hall outside the bedroom. After some hushed phone calls, Andy's family members reemerge, refreshed, Rusty in a tailored navy silk suit, the sister glum but presentable in a pink brocade dress. Her hair is styled into a soft cascade, her prominent face made up in natural colors.

She looks at Will blankly. "Well? Aren't we late for something?"

Will ushers them down the stairs. In the living room, the situation has been explained: Andy's family has arrived at last, better than not arriving at all.

"What about you?" Rusty says to Marion Carroll, who has made a go at the coffee urn in the foyer where the receiving line will be.

"Me?" He places his cup on the fresh white tablecloth, leaving a faint circular stain underneath. "I'm game."

He offers Rusty his arm.

Andy herds them to their seats. The guests are quiet, still cheerful despite the interruption.

The minister continues where she left off, asking if Andy would please now read his vows. Andy takes Will's hand. He says, "I, Andrew Wojak, commit myself to you, Wilhelm Livingston." His voice is quiet, serious.

On his face he wears an open expression, as if behind his eyes a shade has been pulled up in daylight. He runs through a list of remarkable promises, which include cherishing Will and always being honest; knowing he will be braver with a husband at his side.

For a moment Will forgets about the strange little mother and big brooding sister in the back of the room, the man with the woman's name.

The minister blesses the grooms and their life together.

Andy smiles, tilting his head and softening his expression to kiss Will full on the mouth. Everyone claps. As they walk through the crowd, friends tug at their arms and deliver kisses, transforming Will into the bride his mother always feared he'd become.

"Thank you," he says. "Happiest day ever!"

Will's own mother did not come to the wedding; his parents had had him so late in life that now they are too old to travel. This makes him feel strained and attentive around Rusty, technically now his mother-in-law. She steps into the aisle at the very end of the folding chairs, and he imagines thanking her for creating a son who makes his life complete, but she looks exhausted.

Then she catches a scuffed heel on the carpet and stumbles, pitching herself clumsily toward Will's arms. Before he can catch her, she plunges face-first to the carpet.

"Mom," Will says, choking slightly on the word.

Will's own German-born mother does not approve of romance.

"Married?" she said over the phone. "What for?"

Born in Hamburg, she met his father, an American soldier, after World War II. She was working downtown in a U.S. Central Intelligence office, translating Russian messages into German.

She looked like Joan Fontaine, so Will's father asked her to the opera.

"I only agreed to go because it was *Butterfly*," his mother liked to say.

His father, who knew nothing about opera, talked through the entire performance. Over coffee and dessert, he asked for her hand in marriage.

"It was the chocolate cream pie at the restaurant that made me do it," he liked to say.

His mother's version is different: "I married your father because we lost the war."

All Will's life his mother has reminded him that the German people—her people, and by extension his—were the victims of abominable luck and bad leadership. They lost everything: their shirts, their houses, their spirit.

When a war is lost, it's the people who pay.

"We had no choice. And so we were punished. Do you understand what this means?"

Oma worked for the war, but only by sewing buttons on those abysmal brown shirts. *Opa* hid out at home in protest, listening to the radio. According to Will's mother, not a single person in the family—not even a cousin—was a true member of that unspeakable party. Only Will's uncle, a mere boy at the time, was forced against his will to join the Hitler Youth, forced to act as messenger, delivering codes across enemy lines. He rode his bike to deliver messages, scared to death to defy any orders.

"A mere child," Will's mother says. "We were pacifists."

Now, sitting in the living room with Andy's family gathered around to watch them open presents, it comes to Will that his mother's story, the story he has lived all his life is a lie. *Someone did those horrifying things.*

Someone let it happen.

"We brought you this present," A.J. says.

The guests have already made their toasts, eaten cake, danced to the three-piece orchestra. Now most of them are somewhere on the Interstate driving home.

Rusty sits shoeless on the sofa and holds a melting ice pack to her face, courtesy of the two lesbian doctors in attendance at the wedding.

Her lip is swollen, a slight purple bruise beginning to form.

A.J. leans forward. "I'll tell you this, little brother, it was hell getting this thing here."

"Thank you for coming, Alice-James," Andy says. "I know it was a lot of trouble."

Will's mouth goes dry.

"Trouble is only the beginning of what we had," Rusty

says, barely audible through the Ziploc baggie of ice.

"Oh dear," Andy says. "I'm sorry."

Will thinks better of speaking, but says it anyway: "What are *you* sorry for?"

"Willy!" Andy says, but it's too late.

"They barely even got here. Why are you the one who's sorry?"

"Please," Andy says. "They had car trouble."

A.J. says, "Bus, actually."

"Seriously, Andy? You offered to fly them in. You tried to reason with them. They could have come yesterday and been here today. But instead they chose to drive hours through the mountains in the snow, arriving just in time to interrupt everything." Will's voice echoes. The fire crackles and hums in the hearth. "And somehow *you're* the one apologizing?"

"It's been a long day," Andy says, so the others know there's a good reason for Will's irritation. "It's been very stressful planning this wedding."

Rusty shifts her ice pack and raises her hand. Will wonders if he is supposed to call on her.

"We voted," she says. "We wouldn't have missed it. Besides, Bo couldn't stay overnight, and he really wanted to come."

"Bo?" Will says. "Bo isn't here." He keeps himself from sneering at Andy's mother.

"Look here, Wilhelm," A.J. says, "it's not like Andy's been the ideal brother or son, or anything. We did what we could. We got here when we could. It's more complicated than you think."

"Really?" Standing in the middle of the room, the fire roaring at his back, Will keeps his voice level. "Well, thanks for the effort, A.J. You're a real doll."

"Effort? Let me tell you about effort," A.J. says. "Do you

know why Bo wanted to come so badly to your wedding? How about this? Bo is dying. Did you know that, Andy? No, of course you didn't. If you had called us, even once, during the last two years, you might have heard the news. If you had returned one of Ginny's phone calls, but no, not you. Not since Daddy died. You washed your hands and moved on."

Will watches Andy shrink under his sister's gaze, not uttering a syllable in his own defense.

"That's right, Andy: Bo is dying. And we tried to get him here because he loves you, and wants to see you happy. Ginny, too. She's been distraught. She's losing Bo, and he's all she has. Do you have any idea what it's like trying to arrange getting a dying man across state lines?"

No one answers.

"The logistics alone are hell." She looks at Will when she says *logistics*, drawing out each syllable into three small hateful words. Her eyes scour Will's face. "So he's going to die without saying goodbye. And don't you lecture me about effort, Mister Whatever-Your-Name-Is. Andy is the one who didn't make the effort."

Will sits down hard on the sofa cushion next to Rusty, who tucks in her swollen feet to make room.

"I didn't know about Bo," Andy says. "You should have said something."

Andy kneels on the rug in front of the fire near a pile of wedding presents, tears welling in his eyes. Something hot prods Will's ribs.

"Why don't you tell them about all your troubles, Andy?" he says.

Andy leans forward, looking down into the empty "O" his hands are making.

There is only a small window for bold decisions, which can

change the course of people's lives.

"Tell them what's been happening to you these past years," Will says. "What you've been doing that's kept you away from them."

"Listen, here, Wilhelm..." A.J. starts.

Will points at her left elbow for no reason, but she quiets, surprised. "Don't think you can come here, into Andy's home, into *my* home, and take that tone. You're not the boss, here, Alice-James." Her name feels funny in his mouth.

A.J. gets to her feet, but Will steps toward her. Everyone tenses up.

"I don't have to take this kind of abuse," A.J. says.

Will is close enough to see the eye makeup unevenly applied to her left eyelid. He barks out a laugh. "Abuse! Oh, now we're talking! That's just rich!"

A.J. glares at him.

Rusty leans forward to sip her coffee from the good china, careful of her swollen lip. "What's he talking about, Andy?"

"Let's not do this." Andy's voice is soft, a hint of terror in it. *Stop now,* Will tells himself, suddenly sorry to be the one pressing forward.

"What on earth is he going on about, A.J.?" Rusty prods.

"Nothing, Ma."

Something dislodges in the very back of Will's throat, warm saliva moving forward on his tongue—the catalyst for the chemical reactions that make sounds into words and words into meaning. (Or else he is going to vomit.)

"Take it easy, big fella," says Marion Carroll, who is standing in the doorway, drinking what must be his tenth cup of coffee.

Andy stands, struggling to walk over to a chair. "Willy, please."

"But it's not nothing. It's something."

The room is too hot. Will strains forward, watching the fire.

Andy pleads. "Not today. Please, honey."

Will heads toward the bathroom to calm down. As he passes by, Marion Carroll flinches, acting like Will might rush him to make a tackle.

Despite his height and bulk, Will is not the violent type, but these people do not know him.

He runs water from the bathroom sink, splashes his face with the cold, and stands looking at himself in the mirror, his large face red and distorted. His eyes are tired, forehead like a ham hock. This is not the face of his youth. It is an important moment. All moments are, he realizes.

Everything counts, doesn't it?

He opens the cabinet and chooses his weapons.

Rusty sees Will first, tensing her jaw. A.J. stands by the sofa, ready to step forward, if necessary. At Will's approach Andy freezes, shaking his head vigorously back and forth.

"I'll tell you what." Will aims for the sofa with the mother on it. "Just so you know."

She glances nervously at the amber-colored bottles in his fists.

Will can hear Andy swallow in the dead-silent room. "Not this way," Andy says gently, as if Will is the problem.

Will holds one of the bottles above his head. The hand—his hand—swings forward, letting the pills drop into Andy's mother's lap. "ddI," Will says. He flings another at the sister. "d4T." Then he is flinging all the bottles into their laps, the vials of poison keeping the newly married couple alive. "Crixivan! Bactrim!" His voice is no longer calm. "You could have asked!

You could have taken an interest!"

Pill bottles roll in every direction, bouncing off the sofa, spinning toward the curtains, the soft thud of plastic in Will's ears as they bounce against the wall, rattle under the Biedermeier. Everyone in the room watches them come to a rolling stop, settling in a loose constellation where the old wood floor slants in the corner.

Marion Carroll touches one with his toe. "They've made quite a few scientific advances," he says.

For a minute, no one speaks. Then Andy's sister cranks herself up to shout, "Who do you think you are?!"

Will can't hear what she's saying—there is a dull roar in his ears, which turns out to be his voice yelling back at her: "Selfish, selfish people. And you, sister! You ruined his childhood, you made it so he didn't know how to protect himself. You're the one—with your mind games and your…abuse! Do you hear me?"

Andy rises to his feet. "That's enough!"

Will drops the remaining pills. Several lids pop open, bright-colored pills spraying like confetti everywhere. *Stavudine, didanosine, indinavir.*

"You're crazy," A.J. says. She looks at her brother. "He's crazy, this guy!"

The truth is the better heritage, Will thinks, even if it is a borrowed truth. Not Will's exactly, but Andy's family's truth. And isn't Andy now Will's family?

His smile feels like a snarl.

Rusty gets to her feet. To Will's surprise, she limps over to him. "No one tells me anything." She sits on the brick edge of the fireplace, and puts her hand on his.

"Maybe you should pay closer attention." Will is calmer now. "Maybe we all should."

Marion Carroll sighs.

After the war the British came and lived in Will's grandmother's house for eleven years. That's when his mother and father came to America to start their new life. Was that a fitting punishment for looking the other way?

Everyone is quiet now in the room filled with pills.

When the doorbell rings, they are all watching Marion Carroll pour another cup of coffee.

No one moves.

It rings again.

Marion Carroll takes a step forward, but Rusty suddenly recovers: "Don't you dare touch that doorknob."

The front door swings open.

"Ginny!" A.J.'s voice is a mix of surprise and fear. "What did you do with Bo?"

In the foyer stands Andy's missing sister, blue-lipped, teeth clattering, hands raw and ungloved, a lacey covering of snow down her black hair. She is singularly beautiful: a frozen bundle of expectation.

As if an invisible thread were connecting them, Will crosses the room to meet her. As if she feels it too, she looks at him, then rushes in for an embrace. The others stand.

"Is it over?" Ginny can barely speak, shivering in Will's arms. "Did I miss it?"

Andy lifts a blanket from the sofa, and rushes forward to cover them both.

FIRST

IN

LINE

FIRST IN LINE

Ms. LeChance is five years old.

On good days, she waits at the bus stop by herself. Her mother watches a few feet away in a station wagon that is puffing out exhaust. On bad days, Ms. LeChance lies around in her bathrobe, while her mother drinks orange juice and vodka, watches Oprah, and pats her arm. "We're in no mood for kindergarten today!"

Refusing to let life get her down, Ms. LeChance lives by *memento mori*. She mimes asphyxiation because her twin brother Gerald (currently deceased) couldn't get enough air to keep his skin pink and healthy. This was during childbirth. In truth, as babies, they'd both arrived a few months earlier than expected, which caused some complications for little Gerry, whose lungs were not entirely formed.

"Anyway," says Ms. LeChance. "I'm the lucky one, coming out first and getting the air."

Bon Chance, her mother sometimes says.

It's French.

At home, they also speak a little Latin.

Her father says, *Carpe Diem*. It's a philosophy she adores.

At the supermarket, her mother gloats. "My little Mary really wows 'em during Show and Tell!"

In truth, five-year-olds are cruel, and Ms. LeChance is

insecure.

The smell of her need, raw and unfiltered, makes her classmates antsy. No one likes to see a child unmothered.

Driving home with a car full of groceries, her mother makes confessions. "I think the veggie man is awfully sexy." (On bad days, barely a word.)

With their bright puffy jackets and their boxes of organized lunch, the children from the neighborhood seem to know what's what.

The mothers tell them everything: *Poor little Mary and her dead brother Gerry.*

Either way, she lives in the now. "I never let anyone use my *Christian* name," she tells Mimi Schwartz, who is always second in line. "My name is terrible luck and rhymes with the dead."

Mimi Schwartz shrugs her off. "I wouldn't know. I'm Jewish."

A blonde kid with dirty jeans and a black eye gives Ms. LeChance a shove. He is notorious for having five older brothers and a snail collection. Mimi Schwartz offers him a winning smile.

Ms. LeChance cuts her losses. "You can call me Mary-Kay if you'd like."

But no one calls her anything.

Today, she doesn't turn and wave when the school bus comes to take her away.

IMOGENE'S ISLAND OF FIRE

IMOGENE'S ISLAND OF FIRE

OUTSIDE THE BUS STATION, Imogene stood with her mother at the row of wire-slotted vending machines. She put some coins in the one with the cheese doodles and the ketchup-curls.

"Who comes up with such things?" her mother said.

Imogene made an ordinary choice: E-5, potato chips.

"A spinster is a spinster in any town," her mother said, "a no-prize pig."

"Don't worry about me."

She hoisted a pack of paint tubes and brushes over her shoulder, freeing her hands to lift the straw suitcases she'd taken from her stepfather.

"Don't suppose I'd start to worry now," her mother said.

It seemed a hundred years ago since her mother had taught her to be pleasant to men who paid attention—suitors, she'd called them. Even Henry, who was technically Imogene's uncle, her dead father's half-brother, then suddenly her mother's second husband.

Behind the depot, the bus doors heaved open with a mechanical sigh. "Henry says you'll get five miles down the road, come to your senses, and make the bus driver turn back around."

For her entire adult life, Imogene had painted houses for a living and little cards with watercolors on special paper. She was forty. It was time for something new.

"Nothing out there you won't find here," her mother said.

By now the sun was up. A harmless breeze carried the thick muddy odor of the Ohio River.

"I'm going," Imogene said.

When the bus pulled away, she imagined her mother still standing outside the depot, lips pressed together, watching her leave.

It was wonderful to dream of going somewhere new, a place she'd read about in a book. Images of Mingo Junction, now her past, started to fade: the two red traffic lights, renovations at old town hall, farmers carving straight brown lines into the earth with yellow tractors; women at kitchen tables, pouring from pots of coffee; children asleep in their beds. Imogene was leaving the place where everyone resembled everyone else: gaunt and muscular, dishwater-blondes.

"People are horrible, Imogene," Leslie had said. "They don't just accept you. You have to convince them, negotiate, make your own way. You can't just go wherever you want like you're a character in a book."

Leslie, the town librarian, had gotten most of the books Imogene requested from far off collections in Bowling Green and Toledo: Colette, Capote, Stein, Carson McCullers, Virginia Woolf.

"I want to live in the world," Imogene had said.

"The world is not your home, Imogene. The world is unkind."

Imogene had had her fill of Mingo Junction, where an obligatory handwave across the street was as close as she got to people all her life.

During a last wordless night, lying restlessly on top of

the covers, she'd wrapped herself in Leslie's arms and held on tight. Leslie mumbled Earl's name as she drifted to sleep. In the morning, she asked if Imogene would be a bridesmaid at her wedding.

Imogene had almost laughed—the idea of asking her to wear a dress!—then felt like crying.

She hadn't seen it coming.

In the hallway, she'd put her shoes on and found her jacket.

"I'm going to go find something better than this," she said.

"That's just the kind of thing I'm talking about." Leslie sighed. "I want a husband, you want 'something.' You're just so vague, Imogene."

"Love," Imogene said. "I'm talking about going out to find love."

She pictured her mother moving around the kitchen in slow motion. She thought of Henry, who since childhood had been cruel about her books and solitude.

"What kind of Mingo Junction girl are you, Imogene?" he liked to say.

Her father had taught her to be a man. She'd spent her early years trailing him around the farm, learning to pull calves from the muscular insides of their mothers. Imogene appreciated the smell of the blood and the effort that rose from the warm exhausted bodies of the cows, as if they held the secret of life. Her father appreciated her strength and encouraged her natural gifts.

She understood animals better than people.

It wasn't until she'd grown as tall as her own mother that Henry stopped calling her names. After she outgrew Henry, he stopped speaking to her altogether.

"Maybe Henry's just trying to do you a favor, Imogene," her mother had said.

*

Two days, three buses, and a ferry later, Imogene arrived at the place she'd thought she'd never reach. At first glance, the ocean-side community seemed no more than a narrow strip of beach houses lifted off the sand by rotting planks, but the air smelled clean and salty. Her mother's words still ringing in her ears, Imogene hoisted her paint tubes and brushes over her shoulder, picked up Henry's two scratched suitcases, and headed for the nearest bar.

The sign on the door said "Cherry's."

Stepping inside, Imogene saw a wide open space with a dance floor, a jukebox, a few round white tables with matching iron chairs—more like an ice cream parlor than any bar Imogene had ever been in. There were red-and-white-striped curtains and cloth napkins with ribbons on the tables. It was early in the day. Except for an older woman seated under a yellow poster of Marlene Dietrich, the bar was empty.

A barkeep with wide hips and a bow tie appeared in a doorway.

"Name's Cherry," she said loudly. Her thick accent sounded strange. "It's a little early in the season for day-trippers." Imogene could smell the heavy scent of her perfume as she came nearer; it rose above the smoky remains of the previous evening.

"I've come too far for just one day." Imogene dropped her backpack on top of both suitcases, as if she intended to sleep right under the bar. "Some 600 miles."

"You here for the season?" Cherry asked.

"I'm here for forever," said Imogene.

Cherry flashed a wide red smile at Imogene, who suddenly felt stooped with exhaustion. "Only a few die-hards stay year round. But I do hope while you're here, you plan on ordering a drink."

Imogene looked at her.

"Sometime soon would be nice," Cherry said.

Imogene was still standing awkwardly halfway between the door and the bar. "Whiskey," she said quickly. "Is there a pool table?"

Cherry pointed over her shoulder. "In back."

Straddling a striped bar stool, Imogene looked around. "It's pretty in here."

Cherry lowered her voice and leaned in. "Thanks, but I don't date customers."

Imogene's smile was mostly polite. "Too bad for me, then."

Cherry pulled back cheerfully. "It *must* have been a long trip."

"Long life."

Cherry laughed loud and low, posing like an actress, her chin tipped slightly up, "New member of the church?"

Imogene shrugged.

"You'll have to get busy. A lot of hearts to break around here."

"I need a job."

"What's your skill?"

"House painting."

"Plenty of work, too," Cherry said. "You can go down to the end of this dock and find a cheap room for the night, until you get some money. Nice places to rent when you have a little cash."

"I have some money," Imogene said. "Not much."

"You'll do okay." Cherry patted her shoulder. "There's work."

The woman under the Marlene Dietrich poster cleared her throat, nodding at Cherry. Imogene smiled and waved, but got no response.

"Bad place to start." Cherry untied her apron. "Dalia

McGregor. People call her Miss Dale. Lots of money, barely spends a penny of it. She's the oldest woman on the island. Used to be quite a dandy in her time, I'm told."

Imogene watched Dalia McGregor sipping gin. She was dressed in a linen suit, oblivious to the damp Atlantic heat, the shifting sand and stifling sun.

"She looks okay."

"She has one of those outfits in every color, matching shoes," Cherry said. "Sometimes she wears tailored silk pants and smokes a cigar. You should hear her tales about stealing other people's wives, romancing the sisters of her business partners. Claims she had some lawyer's mother once, and a banker's masseuse. Even a nun. Miss Dale says lesbians were better before the advent of the automobile. More authentic."

Imogene flinched at the word. But Cherry was smiling.

"What's the matter, love, you got a crush on old Miss Dale?"

"Send her a drink," Imogene said.

Cherry blinked.

Cherry poured gin into a chilled glass, placing it carefully on a tray, as if it were the first time she'd ever done it. "Going to start at the top and work your way down? Nothing wrong with that."

As Cherry slowly headed for the table, Imogene went to the ladies room to change.

The bathroom was red and powdery. Imogene laughed out loud at a cup of tampons on the basin for the female customers. Henry would have a heart attack. Changing into a paint-speckled navy swimsuit and army fatigues cut into walking shorts, she sat on the john, tying her tennis shoes.

On her way back, she stopped at the pool table to rack up balls for a solitary game. Her mother should see her: making new friends, entertaining herself, not such a plain Jane after all. As soon as she got settled renting a room, she'd send Leslie a postcard telling her not to marry Earl Matthews.

Maybe she'd send Leslie a bus ticket.

Across the room, Miss Dale took a sip of freshly poured gin and scowled.

"Too warm," she said. "Where's the ice?"

Cherry nodded, turning back.

"Wait a minute," Miss Dale demanded. "What's the meaning of this? Who's sending me a drink?"

Cherry studied Imogene's figure by the pool table. "That newcomer wants to stay the season. She's looking for work and a place to rent."

She went to find ice.

"You over there," Miss Dale called out to Imogene. "Come here."

Imogene smiled and approached. "Hello."

A crack in the glass frame above Miss Dale's head lined the edge of Marlene Dietrich's yellow Panama hat.

"Maria Magdalena."

Miss Dale held out her hand. "Dalia McGregor."

"No, I meant Dietrich," Imogene said, taking the old woman's hand. "Her real name was Maria Magdalena, like in the Bible."

Miss Dale waited for her to finish, but Imogene was still pointing at the wall behind her. "You know what Hemingway said about her?"

"Hemingway?" said Miss Dale. "I met the man once—a perfect ass. Most of what he said was rubbish, as I recall."

"He said, 'It makes no difference how she breaks your

heart, as long as she is there to mend it.'"

Miss Dale sniffed the air.

"If I could lie down under that print for the rest of my days, I'd be happy," Imogene said.

"I prefer you not lie down while I'm sitting here," Miss Dale said.

Imogene laughed. "I read somewhere that Dietrich had an affair with this woman, a writer, who at the same time was having an affair with Greta Garbo and Isadora Duncan."

"You read too much," Miss Dale said after a minute. "And if you're speaking of Mercedes de Acosta, I never liked her either."

Imogene's smile faltered.

Miss Dale concentrated on the table. "I'm looking for a housekeeper."

"I'm more of a house painter," Imogene said, "but I know how to use a vacuum."

"I'm getting too old to bend over. My offer is $200.00 a week for light housekeeping. I'll expect you at eight a.m. Mondays and Wednesdays. Fridays noon you can take me shopping. Other errands, when I need them, by appointment, of course."

Her tone made Imogene feel at home, as if she'd become one of the characters in her books.

"Are we agreed?" Miss Dale asked impatiently.

"Only if I can paint your house." Imogene said, "Painting is what I love."

"This is business. No extra money for painting." Miss Dale glared. "You can live in the rental unit round back. It's a mess. I'll let you have what you want and haul away the rest. I haven't bothered with rents and loud tenants for years."

Imogene took in steel-colored curls, black eyes set deep in a round face, magnifying reading glasses perched on her nose.

"Deduct the rent from my pay if you want, but I don't paint for free." Imogene had learned from her stepfather's negotiating style. "You wouldn't want me to. I'll give you a good deal."

"I don't want you to paint." The old woman took a sip and made a face at her gin. Imogene didn't budge.

"I'll think about it," Miss Dale said finally, "but I think slowly."

"Remember Marlene Dietrich in *Blue Angel*?" Imogene said. "Now that was a movie."

Imogene opened her eyes to a musty studio, small and square with a hot plate and a refrigerator. The other side of the apartment was stacked with Miss Dale's boxes.

Imogene had looked briefly through the stacks of books and letters, photographs, and old linen suits.

The night before, she'd fallen asleep on the first page of a book she'd salvaged from a dusty pile, *Civilization and Its Discontents*.

Now, in the tiny, brown-paneled studio apartment below Miss Dale's kitchen in the early morning, she lay on a bare mattress, listening.

She could see through a part in the curtain. Miss Dale's neighbors were men in large, straw-brim hats that sloped off the sun. The daintier one was shoveling peat moss. Miss Dale's dog, an ancient Corgi, danced excitedly at her feet, looking like a little man: short legs and a big face, just like a dwarf.

Most of the time he growled.

"It's a natural reserve," the larger gentleman was saying to Miss Dale. "We should be given something for it. We do own it, after all."

"What a strange thing."

"What's that, Dalia?"

"To think that all these years we've felt the need to own it."

The other man stopped his shovel in mid-air.

Miss Dale gazed into their faces, then stepped back slowly from the fence as Imogene heaved open the filthy sliding glass door and stepped into the morning sun, dressed in a bathing suit and shorts.

"Good morning!"

The men gasped.

"Apparently so," whispered the dainty one.

She stepped quickly across the splintering deck to catch up with Miss Dale and her dog, as they rounded the corner to the front of the house.

"What's the matter, Miss Dale?"

"I simply prefer not to prattle with neighbors," Miss Dale said. "This island is filled with people who think a piece of paper gives them the right to something. And drunken hooligans who come across on the ferry, looking for trouble. I prefer to be alone."

Her first day in Boat Deck, Imogene moved deftly around the ancient beach furniture and knick-knacks, dusting and vacuuming, mopping and shining, tangling more than once with the Corgi, whose name was Pablo Picasso.

The designs for Miss Dale's house hung on the wall, showing how the ends of the house were bowed, the windows shaped like portholes. Just below the architectural blueprints, a sign with large type named it "Boat Deck House." Located on the western end of the island, the structure was shielded from the main thoroughfare—primarily a beer bar, pantry, pizza joint, and a tourist trap with odds and ends for sunbathing.

Miss Dale ordered lunch mid-morning. "Tea and tuna fish."

Imogene wiped the sweat out of her eyes. She hadn't realized she'd have to cook the food she'd bought using Miss Dale's list. She'd thought the old woman liked her enough to make room in her house, but it occurred to her Miss Dale needed someone with her twenty-four hours.

Imogene carried neat plates of food on the tray, wrapping a sandwich for herself and stuffing it in her back pocket. The light was perfect. "I think I'll go down."

"Whatever you like," Miss Dale said.

Picasso barked twice, unenthusiastically, as Imogene packed her paints in a shoulder bag, and ambled down the walkway outside Miss Dale's gate.

It took three weeks to clean away Miss Dale's refuse, to haul the boxes out to the curb on garbage days, to clean the gutters and rake the lawn, which despite attempts to seed it, was mostly sand. Imogene made a home of the stuffy back room, managing to get the hot plate and refrigerator working again. She painted several large watercolors and smaller cards, tacking them to the wall. She wrote postcards to Leslie, tucking them away in a cigar box she'd found among Miss Dale's discarded things.

One evening, Imogene picked at her meatloaf and vegetables as the sky started to fade into a starry evening overhead. Eyeing the old shutters, the peeling white-and-gray paint from the house's trim, Imogene turned to Miss Dale, who was nuzzling old Picasso and feeding him string beans.

The house was finally cleaned up a bit, but she'd grown tired of housekeeping.

"It's time," she said.

Miss Dale followed Imogene's eyes across Boat Deck House. "We'll see about that."

Imogene began scraping the next morning. Preparation was the most important part of the job, Henry had taught her early on.

Paint chips swirled around her ladder.

"It appears to be snowing around Boat Deck," Miss Dale remarked.

"Hasn't been painted in years," Imogene said from her perch on the ladder.

"Hasn't been anything in years," said a passing neighbor over the fence. "Nice to see some activity over here, Miss Dale."

Miss Dale looked out toward the sandy lawn and made a pronouncement: "The deer will overrun the people one day, you know."

"Sure look bad this year."

Imogene had already painted several deer as cards for Leslie, filling out their ribs with smooth brown strokes of paint. Most were scarred and mangy. Imogene had seen the day-trippers feeding them carrots, much to the disgust of Miss Dale.

"The beach erodes terribly every winter," the neighbor said. "Soon there'll be nothing left! I hope the Feds plan on compensating us."

Imogene waited for the conversation to end before resuming her work.

"Strange, isn't it?" Miss Dale said, "I mean, it's very odd."

"What's that?"

"The way things last or they don't."

The neighbor shook his head with a smile, continuing down the length of the fence until it ran out.

Miss Dale clucked her tongue, continuing the conversation in her head.

*

The morning sky slipped into afternoon, spacious and low, while Imogene worked and Miss Dale watched. The sun spread out in a bright blaze like fire. Most afternoons, Miss Dale said she was too tired to go lie down in her room, so she dozed right there in a porch chair near Imogene, supervising the house's makeover.

"There's too much sun out here," Miss Dale complained. She was sitting in the shade with Picasso, who growled in his sleep.

"So go inside," Imogene said.

Miss Dale fretted. "The trees need pruning; the house is going soft. There's more dust than can be wiped away."

"I like to think of dirt as texture." Imogene listened to the distant sound of young people laughing, having fun. An occasional tourist passed, striding across the boardwalks.

"You're not a very good housekeeper, Imogene."

Imogene clung to the top rung of the ladder with bare toes. "I painted some nice cards this morning down by the ocean."

Dale sighed. "Don't change the subject."

Imogene said, "I promise to clean the house when I finish the first coat of primer."

The days crawled by with Imogene on the ladder, slowly relieving the house of its ancient colors, nearly bare. The priming would take several weeks. Imogene found the work difficult without a crew or adequate equipment, but she enjoyed the sunshine and labor.

Miss Dale read in the shade from books in German and French.

Once a week pre-dawn, they took a short walk to the ocean, so Miss Dale could make her assessment of things.

"It makes some people believe in God—this ocean, it's magnificent," she said.

Imogene looked out across the Atlantic; she hadn't thought

about it like that before, but the idea made her feel that she too must have a place in the creation of things. "It's a lot bigger than the Ohio River."

Miss Dale walked precariously, holding onto Imogene's arm as she bemoaned the shortened seashore, the damage of erosion to the beach.

"Hope I last longer than it does," she said. "Looks like someone threw it in the dryer. I remember when it was at least 300 yards of pure sand."

"You've got plenty of time," Imogene said. "Healthy as a goat."

Miss Dale swatted a fly. "This is my last year out here, I can feel it."

"Nonsense." Imogene looked down, smiling. "We'll both be here next summer, and the summer after that."

The sentence circled the air with the insects, buzzing around them.

"In the winter, the island closes down," Miss Dale said. "Everyone leaves, except for a few workmen."

"I'm hearty," Imogene said. "I can keep this place running."

"No need for that," Miss Dale said. "I'll need you in Connecticut. You can stay in the attic."

Imogene dug her bare feet into the beach. "I hate to talk about the summer ending when I just got here."

"Agreed," Miss Dale said. "But I can smell my last summer."

There was no arguing with some people.

"The first time I saw you, you seemed familiar to me," Miss Dale said. "When you're as old as I am you've seen many faces, probably all the kinds there are. You don't think that much about it. But now I realize."

"What's that?" Imogene said.

"It's the stage." Miss Dale thought a moment, shading the

last of the day's sun off her face. "Women don't get much in life. Some get a few hours, if they're lucky, a time when they are exactly who they are supposed to be. It's happening for you now. I can see it. You're turning like a leaf."

Imogene smiled. "I like that."

"It is rather extraordinary," said Miss Dale.

"Did it happen to you?" Imogene asked.

"I was sixty-eight. Can you imagine? After a life bereft of any kind of lasting love, children, acceptance—though not empty of glamour, mind you, and quite a bit of travel—I was getting ready to slow down. Suddenly I could feel it, the pureness of who I was, shining outward for everyone to see. Well, only strangers; I was abroad and alone. A full calendar year almost entirely without witness."

Imogene tightened her grasp of Miss Dale's arm: "I'm glad."

"Unadulterated beauty," Miss Dale said.

One night, while listening to the buzz of mosquitoes outside her room and Miss Dale sleeping just a thin wall away, Imogene heard a ruckus at the front of the house. Thinking it was Picasso taking his nightly prowl, she continued spreading her hand-painted postcards one by one onto the pillow to choose the perfect one for Leslie. She carefully inked a message and read it over several times. The scene on the front had turned out pretty: a long stretch of beach and the ocean ablaze with yellow sun. She hoped to paint many more. One for Miss Dale, maybe. She'd like to know her birthday.

Imogene put a stamp on the other side, addressed the card, imagined herself walking to the post office, but she put it in the underwear drawer with all the others.

Imogene had kept to a tidy schedule: one night a week, sleeping on top of the bedcover on Leslie's large oak frame, which had been hauled many miles from Utica, New York. They'd had dinner occasionally and held hands in the movies. She'd never seen Leslie with her clothes off, though she could imagine it. In fact, Imogene had imagined it so many times she'd worn it down like a sliver of soap.

"What's it like with Earl?" Imogene had asked her.

"What do you mean, *like?*"

In the silence, Imogene understood that Earl hadn't gotten to her yet in *that* way. She wondered how Leslie kept him at bay.

It was a comfort to know, and she snuggled up to Leslie's large bosom and her warm nightgown.

"Never mind," she said, drifting off to sleep.

That was the thing about love: No matter how late it was in coming, no matter the form, you were never prepared. Imogene sprawled on the mattress in Miss Dale's back room. The night was brisk, as if fall were coming sooner than planned. A loud banging and the sound of rolling garbage cans startled her. She sat up in bed, listening a minute, until a few more crashing sounds roused her into action. She pulled her shorts on under a T-shirt, found her flip-flops, and made her way out into the pitch dark.

"Miss Dale?" Imogene called. "Is that you?"

Imogene couldn't see Miss Dale, her eyes still adjusting to the dark. She felt her way carefully toward the front path.

"I'm down here."

Miss Dale was sitting beside the raised wooden front path, down in the sandy lawn where she'd apparently fallen.

"I've hurt my foot." She pulled aside her robe to show her ankle. "I came out to scare away a deer." Miss Dale pointed across to a gnarled pine tree trunk. "I think I've killed it."

Imogene walked over in the darkness, where the baby

deer lay scarcely breathing on a pile of pine needles. Imogene inspected the blood on the doe's face. "Just scratched up."

"Are you sure?" Miss Dale struggled to get a better look.

"She'll be fine," said Imogene. "Let's take care of you first."

Imogene hoisted Miss Dale onto the wooden plank, climbed up herself, and tried to walk with her, but it was cumbersome. She picked Miss Dale up off her feet and carried her toward the house.

"I think it was that cat, Miss Dale," Imogene said, facing her toward the garbage can, where a small orange stray was hissing and spitting, crouched by the side of the house.

"Don't look at the cat!" Miss Dale howled. "It's feral. It will attack. Where's Picasso? Picasso, get in the house. Is Picasso in the house?"

Imogene brought her in through the front screen door. Picasso, safely inside, growled at Imogene until she put her cargo down on the couch.

"Enough, now, mongrel!" Miss Dale scolded. "This Picasso hates other animals like the real Picasso hated people."

"You shouldn't go out in the pitch dark like that," Imogene said. "Old woman like yourself, prowling around. Why didn't you call me?"

Miss Dale's foot was swelling, showing a big purple bruise.

"Phone the fire chief to come get that animal, or we'll be up all night."

"Don't worry about the doe," Imogene scolded. "Let's get you some ice."

Returning with a basin of ice water, she pressed a washcloth to the bruise. "You have to be more careful. Or you'll break your bones." She held out a hand to help Miss Dale sit up. "Put your foot in here."

"Helpless," Miss Dale said. "After all these years, I've

become a helpless old woman."

"Nonsense."

The cold water on her ankle made her flinch.

Imogene steadied herself, preparing to bathe Miss Dale's leg up to the calf.

"I'm going to tell you a secret," Miss Dale said, trying not to shudder. "When I first saw you in Cherry's, I was surprised."

"How come?" She pressed gently. "Does this hurt?"

"From a distance I thought you were a different kind of woman."

"Different how?"

"Frankly, you appeared to be the kind of woman from whom you'd expect nothing"—she paused—"by which I mean, a flat chest."

Imogene's laughter startled the dog, who barked twice and sat back down.

"Oh, you know what I mean," Miss Dale continued. "You're rugged. The dirty blond hair, the boyish tan, the broad shoulders: it all distracts from your womanly figure."

Imogene was embarrassed, but pleasantly so. "Miss Dale, I didn't think you noticed those things."

"One more thing," Miss Dale added. "You have the legs of a worker."

Imogene wrapped up Miss Dale's ankle. "Is that good?"

"Very," said Miss Dale.

"Okay, then. To bed with more ice." When Imogene returned from readying Miss Dale's room, a towel with ice on the bedstand, Picasso was snoring lightly. Imogene put a finger to her mouth. On the couch, Miss Dale was out like a light.

Imogene lifted her easily into her arms, carefully stepping over the dog, and carried her to bed.

*

Gathering rope, a knife, and a pair of rubber gloves from the kitchen, Imogene went quietly down the walkway, stopping twice to look up at the sky filled with chips of light that stretched out over the island. Before she cleaned Miss Dale's house the next morning, she would bring her neatly addressed postcards down to the ocean and set them sailing into the surf.

In the darkness, kneeling down, she felt around the doe's soft coat until she found the crushed bones of its breastplate and a punctured lung, maybe.

She watched fear rise in its gleaming eyes.

"It's okay." Imogene thought about all the animals that had come and gone on her father's farm. She'd watched her father nurse them like a mother, or end their suffering with a quick flick of his wrist.

"Hold still," Imogene said.

ACKNOWLEDGMENTS

Victoria Barrett must be a gift to me from God, for whom I must say thank you. I am so pleased to publish my second book so beautifully with Engine Books. My gratitude also goes to Christopher Schelling, who loved these stories from the get-go; he is a champion of writers, a fierce advocate, and a true believer in literature. I am enormously indebted to Helen Eisenbach for being a great friend and an amazing editor. Her insightful handiwork can be seen on every page and her talent is undeniable. Diane Bartoli gave the book its title, and Maureen O'Neal was right when everyone else was wrong. I worked on many of these stories during a residency at the MacDowell Colony in 1999, and I also owe a debt of gratitude to the W.K. Rose Fellowship, for allowing me to quit my job and write full time for an entire year. Marti Gabriel was there for support through every word. I am grateful to Risa Denenberg for inspiring so many of my stories by telling me hers, as well as to all my sisters from the many writing groups I had throughout the '90s in Manhattan and Brooklyn. Most of all, thanks and love go to Meryl Cohn for being courted way back when with the early versions of these stories—they may not be much, but they're all I had—and for eventually marrying me on the first day it was legal to do so in Massachusetts. You are a wonderful partner in literature and love and an ever-supportive participant in the miracle that is the slowly unfolding short story—which, luckily for me, appears to take a lifetime.

Earlier versions of these stories appeared in the following publications:

"Hands of God" was published in *Bloom Magazine* in 2004.

"Sorry Mrs. Robinson" was published in *The Red Rock Review* in 2002.

"Pretend I'm Your Friend" was published in *Thieves Jargon* in 2008.

"Alice-James's Cuban Garlic" was published in *Seattle Review* in 2005 and was awarded the Seattle Review Fiction Prize.

"A Line of E.L. Doctorow" was published in the *Mississippi Review* in 2004 and was a runner-up for the Mississippi Review Prize.

"Wonderful You" was published in *Eclectica* in 2007 and was a finalist for the *Iowa Review* Fiction Prize.

"Marry Me Quickly" was published in *The Blithe House Quarterly* in 2003 and was named A Notable Online Short Story by The Million Writers Award for Fiction, sponsored by *storySouth*, 2003.

"First in Line" was published in *Quick Fiction* in 2006.

"Imogene's Island of Fire" was published in the *Harrington Quarterly* in 2000.

 MB Caschetta is a recipient of the W.K. Rose Fellowship and the Sherwood Anderson Foundation Fiction Award. Her novel *Miracle Girls* (Engine Books, 2014) received a 2015 USA Best Book Award and an Independent Publisher (IPPY) Gold Medal. *Miracle Girls* was also named a Lambda Literary Award Finalist and a *People* magazine Pick-of-the-Week, where it was hailed as "darkly beautiful."

Ms. Magazine called her first book of stories, *Lucy on the West Coast* (Alyson Books), "a spectacular collection." Since 2007, she has been the anonymous blogger behind the lit-busting literary blog, *Literary Rejections On Display*, which won the *Writer's Digest* 101 Best Websites for Writing in 2014.

Stories from this collection have appeared in *Small Spiral Notebook, Mississippi Review, Del Sol Review, Red Rock Review, Bloom, Thieves Jargon, Ecclectica,* and *Blithe House Quarterly,* among others. Select stories have been awarded *The Seattle Review* Fiction Prize (winner), *The Mississippi Review* Fiction Prize (runner-up), and *The Iowa Review* Fiction Prize (finalist). MB lives in Massachusetts.

In "Hands of God," what does A.J.'s realize about herself and sex when she is with Pedro in Florence? Is it clearer to the reader than it is to her? If so, why?

How would "Hands of God" be different if it were set today instead of in 1973? How would it be the same?

In "Sorry Mrs. Robinson," is Mary-Kay Robinson a sympathetic character? What is she sorry about—is it simply a passing thought she has at a highly emotional time, or is there more to her regret?

In "Pretend I'm Your Friend," what happened to David? Did he kill himself on purpose, or was it an accident?

How does Marie's affair affect her decision-making after David dies? What does she claim is the reason for her attraction to S&M sex with David? What does she tell her childhood friend Susan?

In "People Say Thank You," is Violet Stern really psychic? Or is she merely tuned into the emotions of any given situation?

Why does Violet's mother say: "How do you expect me to keep track of who you are when you don't even know yourself?" Is it a fair assessment of Violet's character?

In "Alice-James's Cuban Garlic," we meet A.J. again about twenty years after "Hands of God." How has she changed? Did she live up to the dreams she had as a child?

What is the significance of the painting A.J. plans to give Andy and Will as a wedding present? What does it represent to her?

How does the family function in "Alice-James's Cuban Garlic"? Why do they vote, rather than reaching a consensus? Why does Ginny go along with it?

Is A.J. more or less of a hero in "Alice-James's Cuban Garlic" than she was in "Hands of God?" How do the two stories speak to one another?

In "A Line of E.L. Doctorow," which (if any) character do you root for? Do you feel differently at the beginning of the story about the protagonist than you do at the end?

In "Wonderful You," we meet Violet (Fields) Stern again, during her summer getaway in Europe. Has her escape worked out? Is she free from her sorrow and her life? What does her traveling companion, Ricardo, mean to her?

What are Ricardo's secrets in "Wonderful You"? Is he really in love with Violet, or are his feelings simply a function of traveling alone and feeling vulnerable and out-of-context?

At the end of "Wonderful You," why does Ricardo kiss Violet? Why does she kiss him back?

How does Ricardo transform at the end of the story? Do you believe he will make his dreams come true? What are they?

In "What's Not My Fault?" we meet Mary-Kay Robinson and her family again. Has she changed? Is she redeemed in the end of "What's Not My Fault?" Do her final thoughts shed any light on whether or not she was truly sorry in "Sorry Mrs. Robinson"?

What is Mary-Kay's experience of dying? What is Lily's experience of her mother's dying? What about Janet's? How are the three women alike and how are they different?

In "Marry Me Quickly," we get an outsider's view of the Wojak family. How does Will see A.J., Rusty, Andy, and finally Ginny?

How does Will's background spur him into action? Does he get to the bottom of things with his new husband's family?

In "Marry Me Quickly" how does Andy compare to how he was described in "Alice-James's Cuban Garlic"? The family thinks of him as an outsider because he keeps to himself, but are the other reasons he feels outside the family?

What is the relationship between Alice-James and Andy? How do we know? From whose perspective do we get the story?

Is Alice James a victim, a perpetrator, or both? Do you feel sympathy for her? Do her siblings have sympathy for her?

Does "First in Line" change your opinion of what kind of a mother Lily (Robinson) LeChance is? Were there clues in the other stories about what she might be like?

How does five-year-old Mary-Kay LeChance cope with her mother's issues? Do you think she will be a survivor like her grandmother?

In "Imogene's Island of Fire," Imogene has an unrequited attraction to Leslie, the town librarian, and then to Miss Dale, the Cherry Grove dowager. How are they similar relationships? How are they different?

Imogene's mother tells her: "Nothing out there you won't find here." Is that true? What does Imogene find?

How does the state of Boat Deck House and its transformation reflect Imogene' transformation? What does it mean when Miss Dale tells Imogene, "You're turning like a leaf"?

In the Book Notes series on *Largehearted Boy*, authors create and discuss a music playlist that relates in some way to their recently published book. Matching a song with each story in *Pretend I'm Your Friend* provided hours of entertainment and exploration, and I have come up with a playlist that will be blaring from my Honda for years.

"SOMEBODY TO LOVE" BY JEFFERSON AIRPLANE

In "Hands of God," an adolescent Alice-James (A.J.) flies to Italy with her best friend and discovers a thing or two about sex, art, and street urchins.

"Somebody to Love" is a trippy song for two would-be flower-children who walk around stoned…a lot.

"YOU LEARN" BY ALANIS MORISSETTE

In "Sorry Mrs. Robinson," Mary-Kay gets disturbing news, but her effort to search her soul goes hopelessly awry.

"You Learn" has lyrics to excuse the worst things you have ever thought, said, or done.

"WE DON'T KNOW" BY THE STRUMBELLAS

In "Pretend I'm Your Friend," bisexual Marie has an affair at work; David, her boyfriend, accidentally shoots himself; and only the cat knows what happened. After that, as you may imagine, everything is kind of fucked up.

"We Don't Know" is an anthem for the young and the lost.

In "People Say Thank You," Violet Stern has a psychic prediction about her own future, which results in losing her husband and planning her escape.

"Fix You" is a haunting tune for the down and out.

In, "Alice James's Cuban Garlic," A.J.'s family crosses state lines in a borrowed school bus to attend a brother's gay wedding, after encountering a little problem with a brother-in-law's brain tumor. Since when has that ever stopped anybody?

"Rise Up" is an inspiring track about overcoming obstacles.

In "A Line of E.L. Doctorow," an au pair gets caught in the competitive sexual snares of a cunning Connecticut couple.

No explanation needed: Redding reinterprets the classic.

In "Wonderful You," a young man falls in unlikely love with Violet Stern, a middle-aged stranger from New Jersey, while in Barcelona on a bus tour. After a stolen kiss, each has a pivotal realization.

Hill croons arousing vocals about love—right, wrong, or just plain incidental.

In "What's Not My Fault?" two daughters struggle to accept Mary-Kay Robinson's final hours, which pass more gracefully than anyone thought possible, including Mary-Kay herself.

The Boss takes on The Byrds, (the bees,) and the Bible.

In "Marry Me Quickly," surprises abound for a soon to be gay-married husband when his in-laws show up late and interrupt the wedding ceremony.

"Take Me to Church" is a catchy, yet dirge-like, devotional hymn…(Can I get an "Amen"?)

"F*CKING PERFECT" BY PINK

In "First in Line," 5-year-old Miss LeChance—Mary-Kay Robinson's granddaughter—is going to have a rough life, isn't she?

This girl will need to listen to Pink's empowering mantra on repeat until she makes it out of childhood, puberty, and possibly beyond.

"FIGHT SONG" (ACOUSTIC) BY RACHEL PLATTEN

In "Imogene's Island of Fire," a woman in her forties strikes out from a small town in Ohio to find her people at the Ocean's edge. Moral of the story: it's never, ever too late for anyone, not even you.

A lone voice croons triumphantly into the wind.

CPSIA information can be obtained
at www.ICGtesting.com
Printed in the USA
LVOW11s2230021116

511335LV00003B/12/P